OLD DOGS

and other stories

Butch Freedman

The following stories have been previously published, and are reprinted here with permission:

"Crybaby" (*Drash*)
"Injuries" (*Rain Magazine*)
"The Yellow Cat" (*The North Coast Squid*)
"Your Life Has Wings" (*The North Coast Squid*)
"An Old Man Surfs" (*The North Coast Squid*)
"A Good Feeling" (*Still Crazy*)
"Insomnia" (*Rain Magazine*)

"Sometimes the pull of our desires is stronger than what would be considered good sense."

—Vera Wildauer

"The only thing I knew how to do was to keep on keeping on."

—Bob Dylan, "Tangled Up in Blue"

Table of Contents

Insomnia

I had always suffered with insomnia, but it had become much worse since the divorce. I hardly slept at all now and never dreamed. I was surprised by how much the break-up shattered me. But the divorce was a good thing. For both of us. Kathy and I had grown apart—a cliché, but accurate. We had stayed together to raise the kids. That was always the excuse. I was 46 when I moved out. Got my own apartment. It was nice enough, lots of space and big windows looking out over a busy street in Northwest Portland.

My first purchase was a new, expensive mattress and box spring. "Money well spent," I told the mattress salesman. He smiled in agreement, glad of his commission. I was primed for that first night's test. The "new beginning" on the line.

Then it started. At first I thought it was traffic noise—a dull vibration. Life in the city. I wasn't going to let it bother me. But the sound grew louder, till I realized it wasn't coming from outside the apartment. It was in the building. I couldn't pinpoint where it was coming from. The apartment below? I knew there were two young women living there. I had seen them checking their mailbox. "Shit," I yelled. "Shit!"

I decided the weird thrumming music (?) was rising up from the apartment below, and so dumbly stomped on my floor. No response. I'll call the manager in the morning, I decided, and went to look for my foam ear plugs. That didn't help, and again I knew sleep was not to come.

The next morning, as I left for work, I found a note taped to my door.

> Dear Neighbor,
>
> We're so sorry about the noise. But we are not the culprits. The awful music bothers us as much as it apparently does you. We've complained to the manager, but he seems unable or unwilling to help.
>
> Apartment 1B

Now I felt like a fool. It was too early to knock on their door and explain my behavior. I told myself I would apologize when I returned home. And I would call the manager, give him hell. I rubbed my eyes. Sleep, dammit. I needed sleep.

The working day passed in a blur. I'm a high school teacher. I enjoy the job—well, most of the time. Every day I teach five classes of 30 or more students. That's a lot of lives, a lot of tender sensibilities to hold.

On my way home after school, I stopped to buy cigarettes at the corner pharmacy. I am planning to quit soon. While there, I impulsively picked up a discounted box of chocolates in a heart-shaped box. A few minutes later, I knocked on my neighbors' door. After a quiet 30 seconds, as I turned to leave, the door opened and there stood one of the young women, looking at me with a touch of suspicion. "Yes?" she said.

"I live upstairs." I pointed.

"Yes?" she said again.

I held out the box of candies. "I'm the idiot who moved into the apartment above you."

"The stomper."

"That's me."

She took the candy, giving it a quizzical glance. "You didn't have to do this."

"I thought the music was coming from down here."

"Because we're young." It wasn't a question.

"Yes. I'm clearly a moron."

She laughed. "Well, not entirely. It was a relief for us to know we weren't the only ones being driven crazy by that weird music."

"Do you know where it comes from?"

"Yeah, though we haven't confronted him. That's why we're glad you're here."

"So I can do the confronting?"

"Something like that."

"And the manager?"

"We call all the time, but he just blows us off. He lives downtown and doesn't want to get involved."

"Great manager."

"You want to come in?" She stepped aside.

I was tempted, but said, "No thanks." And held up my bulging leather briefcase.

"Work?"

"Essays to read." I shrugged. "I'm a teacher."

"Cool," she said. "Well, let's talk again and maybe figure out something we can do about 3A."

"That's the offender?"

"Uh huh. The guy's, uh, eccentric I guess you'd say."

"Anyway, nice to meet you," I said in retreat. "And again, sorry for being a jerk."

"You're forgiven."

After grading papers, I felt exhausted and in need of a deep dream-filled sleep. I turned off the lights, opened a window so the stale cigarette odor could escape. It was quiet now. But within minutes the aggravating noise seeped in through the walls.

It was time to call the manager. He answered after eight or nine rings. "What is it?"

"This is Robert Foreman—in 2B, at The Marlton."

"It's very late, Robert. Couldn't this wait till tomorrow?"

"No, it couldn't." I tried to collect my thoughts. "The music is too loud," I said.

"What are you talking about?"

"The guy in 3A. He plays this weird music all night. I can't sleep. Dammit!"

"Could you lower your voice please?" the manager said. "I'll look into it tomorrow. There's nothing I can do now."

"You could fucking call him up," I shouted.

"I'm not going to do that." He hung up.

The music seemed louder now, like a howling animal. There was only one thing left to do—man up! I put on my shoes and climbed the stairs to apartment 3A. I knocked on the door. When there was no response, I knocked harder.

The door opened a crack. A face peered out. All I could see was one eye staring and a shock of gray hair. "You need to turn the music down," I yelled at the eye. "I can't sleep. You're keeping the whole building awake."

The door swung wider. "So, you're a representative of the entire building then?" I was taken aback by this fellow's appearance. He was old, in his eighties I guessed, with a trimmed white beard, and fully dressed. He was even wearing a tie. "Perhaps some of our mutual neighbors enjoy my entertainments."

"I doubt that." I tried to peer around him. "What kind of fucking music is that anyway?"

"No need for coarse language," the old man said. Then he smiled. "I play the theremin. It's an electronic instrument. You play it in the air." He made a sweeping motion with his hand. "It's my calling you might say."

"Well, it's driving me insane."

"I doubt we can blame that on my playing." He chuckled.

I bit back my anger. "Look, man. It's late. Could you please give it a rest?"

He stared at me for a long moment. "Yes, I'll stop now for the evening."

"Thank you," I said, and took a breath. "Thank you very much."

"Maybe tomorrow you'd like to come back and I can show you how the theremin works."

"Yeah, maybe," I said.

He nodded and closed the door. I went back down the stairs and climbed into bed and soon fell into a dreamless sleep.

The following day at school I felt better, more alert than I had in the past six months. Something had shifted. I breezed through the rest of the day, even found myself smiling and joking with the kids. One of the junior girls told me she was glad I'd "gotten over the grumps." It set me back. "I didn't think you all noticed those things."

"Of course we do." She smiled at me and left the classroom.

When I got back to the Marlton I decided to stop at 1B and catch the young women up on last night's adventure. A different one opened the door. I was glad to be wearing a tie and jacket, assuming I appeared less threatening that way. "Can I help you?" she said after I failed to come up with an opening gambit.

"Uh, I live upstairs. The guy who jumped on your ceiling?"

"Oh. Yes. Teresa told me she spoke with you. We enjoyed the Valentine's day gift."

"Well, I didn't mean it to be a Valentine."

"My name's Andrea." She held out her hand.

I reached out and shook it, relieved that she wasn't angry. "So, I talked to the fellow in 3A. Don't know if you noticed but he stopped playing after that."

"We noticed. It was lovely to have a quiet night for a change."

"Yeah, I had the best sleep I've had in months."

"But you've only been here a few days, right?" She was older than her roommate, and dark complected.

"Yes, but I hadn't been sleeping well before then."

"How come?"

"Long story," I said.

"I've got time." She stepped to one side. "You can come in if you like."

"Uh, sure," I stammered. "That'd be great."

"Well, I wouldn't go that far," Andrea said and laughed.

Their apartment was a mirror image of mine, though more nicely decorated, with a comfortable looking couch and big easy chair. Andrea settled into the chair, and I sat on the couch, let my briefcase drop to the floor. "So, you're a professor, huh?"

"Nothing that grand. I teach high-school English. How 'bout you?" I asked.

"How 'bout me what?"

"Like, what do you do?"

"I read, I write, I go for long walks without knowing where I'll end up. I also collect frogs, ceramic ones."

"I meant, what do you do for work?"

"Oh that. I don't let my work define me. You know what I mean?"

"Sure. I don't really define myself as a teacher either. It's what I do to support myself."

"So, how do you define yourself?"

"Still trying to figure that one out. Guess you could call me a life-long seeker."

"Is that what I should call you then? Seeker?"

"My friends call me Buddy." I took a breath. "So, you're not going to tell me what you do for work?"

"I work at an architectural firm, do the renderings for commercial buildings."

"You're an artist."

"I'm a wage slave."

"What do you really want to do?"

"Buddy, we've only just met." She laughed.

"I want to write books," I muttered, something I hardly ever revealed.

"So why don't you?"

"I don't have the time. What with teaching and grading papers, and not sleeping." Andrea didn't say anything, just kept looking at me. "I know, I know. That's just bullshit. If I wanted to do it I'd find the time."

Still, she said nothing.

"It's on my agenda. Soon." I reached down for my briefcase. "I'd better get going."

"You know, it's okay to be confused," Andrea said then.

"We just met." I stood up to leave. "And here I am telling you all my secrets."

Andrea stood then also. "I'm guessing you've got a lot more secrets to tell."

"And you?"

"Yep, I've got a few. Let's talk again some time."

"Let's. I'd like that."

I felt better, and so decided to go for a walk, pulled on my sneakers, and headed out. I hadn't had much chance to explore the neighborhood. As I walked briskly down Northwest 21st, I took it all in—the coffee shops, taverns with outdoor seating, a Thai restaurant, a barber shop where three lady barbers were snipping away. There were lots of young people around, but also a sprinkling of older types, ex-hippies and other eccentrics. I wondered if I now fit into that category. As I walked farther north, I found myself in a sprawling urban park and followed the first trail into a forested landscape. I walked for miles.

On my way back to the apartment. I stopped and bought some groceries—eggs, a loaf of crusty bread, a hunk of gouda cheese, mushrooms, a few other vegetables. I'd make an omelet for dinner. I also bought a cheapish bottle of red wine.

The phone rang as I was putting away my supplies. I was surprised. I hadn't had any phone calls since I'd moved in. "This is Victor Charles," the voice on the line said.

I racked my brain for a connection. "I'm sorry, do I know you?"

"After a fashion. We met last evening."

"Last evening?"

"You assaulted my front door."

"The theremin guy?"

"Indeed. The very same."

"What can I help you with?" I didn't want to be rude, though I was hungry and anxious to open my bottle of wine.

"We never did meet properly. I'm afraid I don't even know your Christian name."

"It's Robert, and it's not Christian," I said.

"I meant no offense," Victor said. "I'm a bit of a dinosaur as you no doubt noticed."

"It's fine. People call me Buddy, though."

"But Robert is a fine name just as it is. Would you be offended if I called you that?"

"Sure, whatever."

"I was hoping you might join me for dinner. I thought you professed some interest in learning about the theremin."

"Did I?"

"Perhaps I was mistaken," Victor said. "It certainly wouldn't be the first time."

"I was just about to make my own dinner," I told him. "It's been a long day."

"All the more reason to let me attend to you."

"What the hell," I said. "I'll bring a bottle of wine."

"Splendid," Victor Charles said.

◊ ◊ ◊

Before I headed up to the old fellow's place, I took a couple hits off an old joint. Figured I needed a little jolt to keep going. I grabbed the wine and climbed up the staircase. The hallway smelled musty, like sawdust and old memories. I heard the eerie music before I reached Victor's door, though much softer now. I stood there listening for a moment. Weird, like music from a different dimension. I knocked and the wailing music stopped. Victor opened the door, still dressed formally, three-piece suit and tie.

"Welcome Robert, welcome," he said. I realized then I was a bit too stoned. I wasn't used to getting high anymore. I barely knew where I was and had to stop for a few deep breaths before I crossed the threshold. "Are you okay?" Victor asked.

"Yeah, I'm good." I looked around the apartment, trying to take it all in at once; old, heavily upholstered furniture filled every corner, and dozens of photos and paintings covered the walls. I wanted to go look at each one but felt that would be impolite. Instead, I headed to what was clearly the focal point of the main room. "This is it, then?" I asked, and stared at the long, polished wood box.

"Yes, that's my theremin. Would you like to see how it works?"

"Sure, but there aren't any keys," I said, imagining it to be some sort of organ or piano.

"No need," Victor said, stepping behind the machine. He flipped a switch and began slowly waving his hands between the two metal posts rising from the base. A strange, eerie music wafted into the air, clearly controlled by the rising and falling motion of Victor's hands and fingers. It was as if he was pulling music out of the air.

"This is fucking beautiful," I said.

"Thank you," he said, while he continued to draw strange melodies from the box.

I was entranced, wanted to lie down on the carpet and drift off.

"Let's open that lovely wine now, shall we?" He dropped his arms, and the music ceased immediately.

"Yeah," I said, returning to earth. "I think I need it."

Victor radiated a sort of peacefulness, which I found infectious. He had prepared a whole chicken and roasted vegetables, which he served on heavy white plates, with folded cloth napkins, and real silverware alongside. He poured the wine into crystal goblets.

"I feel so well-taken care of," I told him, while digging into the sumptuous meal.

"It's my pleasure," the old man said. "As you might imagine, I very rarely have company."

"No family?"

"None to speak of. My wife died some years ago. We never had children. A decision we both thought best, though now I sometimes wonder." He smiled and looked off above my head.

The wine tasted better after the second glass. "What do you do other than play the theremin?"

"You mean, what value do I have left in the world?" He smiled, so I knew he wasn't angry.

"I meant, it must be hard getting, you know, old?"

"It is, indeed, difficult, Robert. Every day is a struggle against the ravages of an aging body. I won't go into the details. But I do try to appreciate whatever time I have remaining."

I took another swallow of wine. "How do you do it? I have a hard time getting out of bed in the morning and I'm in my forties."

"A good age," Victor said. "You should treasure it."

"I guess."

"One must always do the things that makes one happy."

"How the hell do you do that?"

"Of course, it isn't easy. This world of ours can be an ugly place." Victor stood then and began to clear the dishes.

"Look, Vic, I better go back down to my place now. Need to get some sleep."

"Before you go, may I show you something?" He stacked the dishes neatly in the sink.

I stood up, felt a bit dizzy. "Sure, what?"

He walked into the back room and motioned for me to follow. "I have to get up pretty early," I called out to his back. "Faculty meeting."

Victor bent over and pulled a heavy cardboard box from beneath his bed. He stood up slowly, trying not to let me see him wince. I plopped down on the bed. He opened the carton, shuffled around some photos and books, then pulled out a yellowed paper, which he carefully unfolded, then held out to me. "What is it?"

He came to stand beside me, his head just above my shoulder. "These are my release papers."

"Release from where?"

"From the camps. From the Nazis." He smiled, almost apologetically.

"Oh man, I didn't even think you were Jewish. You asking me about my Christian name and all."

"I'm not Jewish," Victor said. "Now I follow no religion, but when we were detained, my family was Catholic."

"So, why'd they, uh, detain you?"

"The Gestapo discovered that my parents were sheltering a Jewish family. That was almost as bad as being a Jew. Maybe worse, in their eyes. They tore apart our home, then shipped us all off. It's an old story now."

"Damn," was all I could come up with. "Jesus fucking Christ."

"Exactly," Victor said. Then we both looked at each other and laughed, because there was nothing else to do.

We spent another hour or so discussing his experiences at Dachau. And I told him about my Eastern European Jewish heritage and all the relatives in Poland and Hungary I never got to meet. I thought it strange that his reminiscences weren't tinged with anger or despair. The old man talked mostly about the friends he had made in the camp and the way he had been accepted by his "Jewish brothers and sisters." "Every day we survived was a gift," he said.

"I would have wanted to kill somebody. Didn't you want revenge after you were liberated?"

"At first I did."

"Then what?" We were both sitting on the bed now, the box of memorabilia between us. Every few minutes, he would pull out another photograph or newspaper clipping and pass it to me.

"I realized pretty quickly that my anger was not going

to help me get on with my life." He smiled then. "I must sound like a terrible Pollyanna."

"No, I just don't understand how you managed to stay, I don't know, joyful?"

"Yes, that is exactly the word, Robert. Joy. It's what we all need no matter the circumstances. Even for a moment, even a fraction of a moment." He took a labored breath. "I hope you are finding some joy in your own life." He put his hand on my shoulder. I started to choke up.

"I better go home now," I said when I regained my composure.

"Tomorrow then?" Victor asked.

"Tomorrow what?"

"We'll go for a stroll? Talk some more? Have a coffee?"

"Okay," I said. "Would you mind if I brought a friend? She lives in the building."

"That would be lovely," Victor said, as he opened the door for me.

As I made my way down the steps, I heard the strange vibrations of the theremin once again. This time it made me smile. By the time I unlocked my apartment door the music had stopped. He's accompanied me to my room, I thought. That night the dreams returned.

Old Dogs

The Golden Lab across the street whines every morning at 6 a.m. I know because I wake up then and look at my alarm clock. I've spoken to the owners about this disruption, but they are not taking the situation seriously. Felix, they tell me, is still a puppy. He thinks we're never coming back when we put him outside. Then they laugh. He'll get over it eventually, they say.

Okay, I say, it's no big deal. I have to get up anyway. This is not true. I don't have to get out of bed until I want to. I'm retired and I like my sleep. I worked hard all my life and now I want to sleep in on occasion. Is this so much to ask? But I don't say this to Harry and Maria, the young couple who are the owners of Felix, the puppy who I'm starting to hate.

Don't get me wrong, I don't dislike animals. I am, in point of fact, a dog owner myself. People need their pets, I say. There is no better companion than a dog, or even a cat. But my dog, Lucky Lou, doesn't wake the whole neighborhood at 6 a.m. every damned day of the week. I will obviously have to take stronger measures with these people and their fancy puppy.

Once I'm up, there's no point in trying to get back to sleep, so I make myself a strong cup of coffee, take all my medications, and go out into the backyard to have a cigarette. Yes, I smoke. Big deal. So I'll die five years sooner and not be a burden to my children, who are all grown and not so crazy about me anyway. If I moved to Italy or Spain, or even Israel, nobody would care if I smoked an occasional cigarette. People there are more tolerant of certain vices. That's what I'm told anyway. I've never been.

I read the *Philadelphia Inquirer* next. (Yes, I still get the print version.) I check the sports pages first. That's a habit from my youth when sports were everything to me. And the only way I was able to connect with my father, who was a gruff and silent man. Still, he would talk to me about the Phillies and the Penn football team. We had that. The most interesting articles in the sports pages these days are the crime notices. Professional athletes are always beating up their girlfriends or driving down the freeway in the wrong direction at three in the morning, and worse stuff too I won't even talk about. Why these things interest me I couldn't say. Maybe my therapist could explain it. That's another whole story—this therapy business. My ex-wife is the one who got me started on that. She said I needed to get in touch with the roots of my conflicts. What roots? I said. What goddamn conflicts?

You're an angry man, Buddy, she said. It's ruining our marriage.

Am I the only one here with problems? I said to her. But I ended up going to the therapy. Now, once a week I pay this kid half my age a hundred and fifty dollars to have a conversation about my *issues*. I could get the same thing for free at the neighborhood bar. But I go anyway because, to tell the truth, I've started to like it. After all, for almost an hour, all we talk about is me. I've never had that before. And the doctor—George is his name; George Lewinski, PhD—he genuinely seems to care. And I don't think he's patronizing me, being nice to the old man. When the situation calls for it, this boy can be damn hard, steely, even when I'm in tears. Which I usually am by the end of the session. I'm not ashamed to say it. I've had a difficult time in my life and George has helped me to see why that was and still is and how to keep going and have compassion for myself—and others.

While I'm doing all this therapy and feeling better, my wife runs off with a man ten years her junior and says to me only, sorry, Buddy, but this new fellow is a doer, you're a complainer.

For Christ's sake, I yelled after her, that's what I'm working on.

I throw the sports pages down. The Phillies are not

going to make it to the Series—again. I don't care so much anymore. It's just a game. Isn't everything?

I've got to move along now. Take a shower, eat breakfast, walk the dog. It's a routine I have. Sometimes I think routines are all I have. But I won't let myself get side-tracked with negativity. George says I need to treat my moodiness as a disability. He says I should learn to accept it just like a guy who loses an arm in an auto accident has to learn to live with that. What I say to George, Mister PhD, is I'd rather be missing a limb. Cause I could always get one of those artificial ones, a prosthetic device. Your feelings, those are not so easy to replace I tell George. Still, Buddy, you have to go on living, he says. Do the best you can. Be kind to yourself. And I could do that, I say. I could, if it wasn't for that damn dog who won't let me sleep. It's the puppy that's the problem. George shakes his head. He looks sad.

I decide to write a letter. This way I can be more logical. Not get so angry or flustered. Present my concerns in a clear, forthright way. I've always been quite breezy with the written word. I sit down at my desk and take out a fresh piece of stationery.

> Dear Harry and Maria (sorry I don't know your last name).
>
> This is your neighbor Bud from across the

street. As you may recall from our previous conversation, I have some serious concern about the noise your fine dog Felix is making at a very early hour. I know it is a difficult task to properly train an animal and I respect your reasons for putting Felix out of the house. (Sometimes the sun is not even up.) Dogs have to learn to fend for themselves, just as we human beings do. But perhaps you are unaware of the great din that the puppy creates in the neighborhood with his pitiful whining. I imagine you two go back to bed in your upstairs bedroom (not that I know where you sleep, never having been invited into your home) and with the thick walls and insulation these new houses have you don't even hear the animal's howling. I can assure you, though, that I, your neighbor, do hear poor Felix. My house is old, like me (ha-ha) and my bedroom is on the street side. What I am hoping is that we can be good neighbors and that you will consider keeping your puppy inside the house until a later (decent) hour. Perhaps nine o'clock?

Sincerely, Your Friend and Neighbor,
Bud Shore

That should do it, I think. I seal the letter in an envelope and walk it across the street to Harry and Maria's mailbox. Reasonable people can work out their differences. I am learning to be more compassionate, I tell myself, and hope that these neighbors of mine feel the same.

The next morning I am once again awakened by the barking dog. I stumble out of bed and rush to the front door, to do what I am not sure. But I find a letter left on my doorstep alongside the morning paper. See there, I say to Lucky Lou, as I bring the envelope into the house, action begets action. Lucky is spread-legged on his doggie bed. He doesn't move off that bed very often these days. He's arthritic, the vet tells me, and half-blind and I don't know what I'll do when he passes. I'm too old to start over with a new dog.

This is a letter from those people across the street, I say. They are responding, you see. I hold the letter above my head and pump my fist. Lucky Lou opens one eye to see what all the fuss is about, then lets it close. I prop the letter up against my juice glass on the kitchen table and go about fixing my coffee and toast. I like real butter and orange marmalade with my toast. This is my breakfast ritual. George says it's good to have rituals. Not that George knows everything in the world. He's just a kid, not even thirty-five and probably pulling down two-hundred thousand a year or more even. What does he know about struggling through a life where everyone leaves, where even the damn dog is dying.

I gaze at the envelope while I'm enjoying my first sips

of coffee. My father, who never talked much, did say to me once when I was a boy and hurrying through my breakfast so I could go out and play with my friends: Slow down, boy, life won't stop without you. I didn't know what he meant by that. Was it okay to miss out on playing stick-ball with your buddies while you were stuck in the house staring at the table? But I didn't ask him to explain. That would have made him angry. And nobody liked it when my father got angry.

I will open the letter in due time. The anticipation is delicious. Small joys, small joys. My father might have said that also, though he was hardly a joyful man. George says that many of my current conflicts stem from an unresolved relationship with my father. That's how it was in those days, I tell him. Fathers didn't talk. They went to work, came home, and expected dinner to be on the table. And if you were a kid and didn't want to get smacked, you kept out of the way. What's so unresolved? From all I could see my father didn't much like me and I was scared to death of him. George thinks I am making a joke. So I tell him the story of how my father decided to take me and my brother to a Phillies' game at Connie Mack Stadium. We were so excited we couldn't even eat our breakfast. I spent all morning rubbing neatsfoot oil into the pocket of my mitt in case a foul ball came my way. Finally, it's time to leave and Sammy, my little brother (dead now), and me climb into the back seat of my father's Buick.

It smelled like the cigars he smoked. Sammy is jumping up and down. He's too young to even know what's happening except that it's special and Mom isn't allowed to come. I try to tell him to calm down, that Dad is going to get angry, but Sammy is somewhere beyond all that. He is wearing a cub scout hat, the closest thing he has to a real baseball cap like my red Phil's hat.

We're going to the game, we're going to the game, Sammy chants as he bounces up and down so hard that the whole car is rocking.

I am saying, sit down already. Shut up, you idiot. Dad is going to kill us. But Sammy keeps jumping, his head almost hitting the roof of the car. I move quickly to the other side of the seat when I see Dad yank open the car door. Without even a word, he backhands Sammy across the face, knocking his scout cap off his head. My brother crashes over on top of me already crying.

Stop that crying or I'll give you something to really cry about, my father yells. I try to get Sammy to stop. I hold his head tight to my chest and just like that he falls asleep. I think for a moment that he has died. But I can feel his breath on my face. I don't even remember who won that game. No foul balls came my way. I know that much.

I take the last sip of my coffee and wipe my mouth with a cloth napkin. Why not? They can be washed, so why waste money on paper? It's time to open the letter. My first disappointment is the paper itself, yellow notebook stuff, with the edges torn. I unfold it and read:

> Hey Bud,
>
> Sorry about Felix's continued barking. But I'm afraid that's what dogs do. We believe in non-intrusive and non-violent training. A pup doesn't learn anything by being punished except to fear his owners. We want a healthy relationship with our pet. As a dog owner yourself, we're sure you'll understand. By the way, where is Lucky Lou these days? It shouldn't be many more weeks before Felix comes to understand and self-correct his behavior. Let's all just take a breath and stay cool.
>
> Your neighbors,
> Harry and Maria Chance

Not many weeks! Stay cool! I crumple up the letter and throw it toward the trash can. I feel like screaming or punching a hole in the wall. But I take a deep breath instead. I need to stay in control, need to figure this out. It's not worth having a heart attack over. There are other ways to deal with this issue. Breathe, I need to breathe. George says I should breathe deeply when I am upset. Three breaths in, three breaths out, he says. Close your eyes and concentrate on a soothing color. Pretend you are at the beach on a breezy summer day. George talks like this. I don't always listen.

Goddamn them anyway! If this is the way these people want to play the game, then so be it. I know how to handle this. Come on, Lucky Lou, I call out. Time for our walk. Lucky gets up slowly and stretches out his front paws. He's not so old that he doesn't still enjoy our morning walks. I get his leash out of the closet and take down from the storage shelf a box of D-Con pellets that I bought for the mice that I heard scampering about in the basement. I then mix some of the pellets into a ball of raw hamburger and slip the cold meat into my jacket pocket.

When Lucky and I come out onto the sidewalk, Felix stops his whining and rushes to the front of his yard to greet us. He's a good-looking animal, bouncy and silly like all puppies. Lucky Lou pays him no attention. He's sniffing around for a good place to have his morning bowel movement. I take the poisoned hamburger out of my pocket and stoop to slip it under the fence. This will take care of the problem, I say to myself. But then Lucky Lou barks. And begins to growl at me, the hackles on his back rising in a way I have never seen before. The puppy yips, runs around in happy circles. I draw back my hand and slip the meat back into my pocket. Lucky Lou stops growling. I'm sorry, I say, I am so very sorry, though I'm not sure who I'm talking to. Is it Lucky? Or Felix? Harry and Maria? George?

My ex? My father? Or myself? The answer seems clear. I've got to do better. I reach over the top of the fence and Felix jumps up to playfully nip at my fingers. I glance up and see Maria watching us through her window. I wave at her, and she smiles and waves back. I pull on Lucky's leash. Come on, old fella, I tell him, let's walk while we still can. It's going to be a good day.

Carpentry

Donny was a junkie. He was also a damn good artist, and a finish carpenter—that's how he made enough money to sustain a heavy habit. I guess you'd have called him a functional addict. But the junk always came first. And last. I'm no one to judge. I had my own problems then. And, I'll admit, I sometimes joined Donny shooting up. Okay, it was more than sometime. A lot of times, really. Until I got a cyst on my arm the size of a baseball and got scared that I was going to die if I kept up that shit, so quit—cold turkey. It was miserable. Like having a severe flu combined with a waking nightmare, but I had a friend then who made me believe I still had stuff to live for. I made that choice. Donny never did.

I tried to get him to kick, but he just gave me a sad grin, and went on sharpening his chisels. Donny never talked much about his past. Junkies live in the present. They do have that going for them. "Where can we score?" was often the extent of our conversations. Still, we were friends—at least I thought so. On some level that didn't require talk, we understood each other. Understood we were both broken. Maybe irretrievably so. There was a world out there that we didn't fit into, so we made a small space for ourselves inside an old house.

I'd been pretty straight up till the time I met Don. Sure, I'd done my share of drugs, but mostly the recreational types. A lot of pot and LSD, stuff that expands the old brain pan. Made us counterculture types think we were something much more special than it turned out we were. I think we were mostly just putting off adulthood as long as we could, cause being an adult, judging by our parents, was not a good place to be.

Thing is, once I graduated from college, tried graduate school, and a misguided long-term relationship, I was looking for something that would take me down a different road. I didn't know it at first (you never do), but what I was searching for was oblivion. I wanted to be wiped away. And that's exactly where my first hit of heroin took me. It took me lots of places after that, most of them bad, but I'm getting ahead of the story.

I had travelled out to Aspen, Colorado after that relationship fell apart. I remember throwing a plate of spaghetti and red sauce against the wall of our dark city apartment and watching it slide down in a blood-red smear, after which my girlfriend correctly told me to "get the fuck out, asshole, and never come back." So that's what I did.

I called a guy I'd hung out with in grad school in the early seventies, who had moved out to Aspen and bought a falling-down Victorian, which he was planning to rehab and sell for a big profit to one of the nouveau-riche ski fucks who were just beginning to populate that town and, in the process, driving real estate prices through the roof. "Come on out, man," he told me. "I'm about to get fucking rich."

The problem with this flipping houses scheme was that my friend, Perry, didn't know shit about carpentry or any other building related skill. Hell, we'd both been MFA students. We might be able to write about houses, but we sure as shit couldn't build them. That's where Donny came onto the scene. A local character (as Perry first described him to me), he needed a place to crash and made a deal with Perry to work on the house in exchange for being able to stay in the dilapidated old building. It worked out—for a while.

Perry told me, when I arrived in Aspen, that he'd put me to work swinging a hammer and I could stay in the house with Don. "Fine with me," I said. Physical labor sounded like what I needed then. Something to bleach the city life and my own failures out of my bones. Turned out I was right about that. I loved framing out a wall, driving nails, even carrying sheetrock up three flights of stairs, then nailing it into place while Donny showed me the tricks and tools of the trade. He loved that old house, admired it. First thing he showed me were the original architectural plans, unrolling sheets of cracked and aged drawing paper. God knows how he came up with those. For a couple months there we banged it out, made good progress. Perry was happy; he told me that maybe I could even be a partner on the next house, but I didn't believe him. The guy was a total bull-shitter. All talk mostly. But you can go a long way on big talk. It's a skill I never learned. I was stuck with saying what I thought, and mostly avoiding people. My ex had called me a misanthrope. "You mean honest?" I said.

She shook her head, "Grow up, Buddy."

Donny and I were supposed to start work on the kitchen when I walked into his room that morning and found him sprawled in his narrow bed, fully clothed, a spike in his arm. I figured right off he was a dead man, but still I tried to rouse him, shook him by the shoulders, pulled the empty syringe out of his arm. Nothing. I didn't want to do CPR on him, but knew I had to. I held his nose closed and blew into his mouth. "Get up, motherfucker," I yelled, then blew in again. The vomity smell was almost unbearable. I stopped and pounded on his chest. I didn't know what to do, but I didn't want him to die. Shit, he was my friend, dammit. I thought about calling the EMT's, but the old house didn't have a phone. "Donny," I screamed and punched him in the chest again and again. "Wake the fuck up, man!"

And then he did, his eyes fluttered open and he sat up, ran a hand through his greasy hair. "What the hell are you doing?" He looked pissed off, and balled his fists up, like he was about to swing at me.

"You OD'd, man. I thought you were fucking dead. I just saved your stupid ass."

"I'm fine," he said, and swung his legs off the bed. Hitched up his pants. "Got any coffee?"

"You're not hearing me," I said. "When I came in, you were a dead man! I had to give you fucking CPR."

"Yeah?" Don blew his nose into a soiled kerchief. "How was it for you?"

"Disgusting. Next time I'll let your skinny ass die."

"Wish you would," he said, and grabbed up his tool belt. "Now, how about we get to work?"

I thought about quitting then, didn't want to be around for that next time. I didn't dig Aspen anyway, and Perry was starting to get on my nerves, always bugging me about why this or that wasn't getting done on time and complaining about running out of money like it was somehow my fault. Most weeks I wasn't even getting paid. "Who needs this shit?" I asked myself out loud. I was sitting at the counter of the local breakfast place—The Corral—and the waitress filling my coffee cup nodded, like she knew what I meant, which she probably did. I smiled wearily at her. "Sorry," I said. "Having a bad day. Actually, a whole bunch of bad days."

"Been there, honey. Don't worry. It'll pass—or maybe it won't. You never know."

"Gee, thanks for the pep talk." We both laughed then, and I felt somewhat better.

"I think I have to split," I said.

"You haven't even gotten your eggs yet."

"No, I mean like get out of town. Things aren't working out here."

"How long you been in Aspen?"

"About four months, maybe more. Kinda losing track."

"Give it a chance. The place can grow on you." She smiled at me, and I looked up at her. She was younger than I first thought, tall and thin, with dark, almost black hair, and eyes that matched, a longish, hooked nose; *aquiline*, I think they call it. There were lots of other customers waiting for their plates of eggs and biscuits and the cook was ringing his little bell for her to pick up orders, but she stayed right there, waiting. I didn't know for what. "You ever go hiking?" she asked.

"Not really. Not here anyway. I'm from back East," I said, and immediately felt foolish.

"Well, no wonder you don't like it here. You're not taking advantage of the real Aspen. You know, not the tourist shit."

"That could be," I said, not wanting to let go of my misery.

"You wanta try?"

"What do you mean?"

"Hiking. Isn't that what we're talking about?"

"Sure, yeah, I want to go hiking." I took a sip of my now lukewarm coffee and tried to figure out what was happening.

"Cool," she said. "I'm done with my shift at three. Come by then. Wear some good boots."

I started to tell her that I didn't own any hiking boots and didn't even know her name, but she was gone, off to pick up her plates and to talk some shit with the short-order guys in the back. When she came back with my over-easy eggs and bacon, all she said was, "Want hot sauce?"

"Yes, please," I told her.

Found out when I came back that afternoon that her name was Sully. I told her mine was Robert. "But call me Buddy. That's what my friends call me."

"How about if I stick with Robert," she said. "Don't want to shortchange you. Your mom gave you that name for a reason, and where are your damn boots?" She pointed to my high-top Converse.

"Don't have any. Where we going anyway? You know,

I'm a little out of shape." I wasn't about to tell her about the smack. Or that I hadn't gone hiking in a long time— like probably ever.

"Don't sweat it." Sully looked me up and down. "You'll be fine, Robert." I could feel how she was trying out my name. I liked the sound of it, like I was back with family. Then she stared at my Cons. "Damn, did you have to get red ones?"

I wasn't sure if she was joking. Figured it didn't matter, then followed her out of the diner and kept right on following, up into the green, cool mountains surrounding the town, panting, unable to catch my breath the higher we got, and Sully kept turning around to smile and ask if I was okay, and I wasn't about to tell her I needed to stop, even though my lungs were burning and my knees screaming. But eventually we made it up to the peak, where even though it was still summer there was snow on the ground. We stopped briefly to look at the scene below us, which I had to admit was breathtaking. That's the word I used, cause I couldn't come up with one that really captured how I felt that my life was changing right then and there. Maybe I should have just said that. Finally, we made it back down, which wasn't much easier than the going up part. "I never did anything like this before," I admitted then, feeling both out of breath and elated.

"Yeah, no shit," Sully said. "So, now what do you think of Aspen?"

"Not bad," I said, between wheezes. "I may start to

like this." I waved at the surrounding mountains, but I was mainly thinking about Sully.

"What'd I tell you?" Then she snorted a laugh.

My life in Colorado changed after that. I mean, it's not like I fell crazy in love, but more like some other door opened for me, and I didn't have to keep going back to that same old shitty place where all I wanted to do was shoot up or run away. And in the next few weeks I told both Perry and Don about Sully. Well, I didn't really have to tell them. Aspen was a small town then and everybody knew everybody else— especially since most all of us ate breakfast at The Corral, and because Sully came by our work site to pick me up most days after her shifts. Donny was impressed—and he was a hard man to impress. He mostly kept his head down, but I could tell he liked Sully. I think he could see that she wasn't afraid of him, and always had something to say to him, smart shit, and even asked to see some of his paintings, which, surprisingly, he showed her. I mean, Donny didn't show his work to hardly anybody. It took me a month of asking before he let me look at some of them, which I thought were brilliant—oil paintings of weird landscapes, barren deserts, breaking waves, tumbleweeds and cacti, but never people. I asked him where he'd learned to paint, but he only shrugged. "Taught myself." Later, he gave me one of those paintings. I tried to pay him for it, but he wouldn't take my money. "Ain't no big deal," he said.

"I think it is," I said, standing back to admire the work, a roadside billboard, with the words, SEE HERE NOW painted in bright blue letters. I still have it hanging on my wall. It reminds me of Donny and that whole sad and lovely year every time I look at it.

When the house remodel was only half-done, Perry showed up saying he wanted to talk to us. Don and I came out on to the front lawn to meet with him. "What is it, man?" I asked.

Perry rubbed his hands together. He was a handsome cat, even I had to admit, tall, slicked back black hair, white teeth, a fucking movie star profile. He was good with people, a charmer—till you really got to know him. "I think I've got a buyer for the place." He flashed a toothy smile. "They're willing to pay all cash. No inspection or anything. Only one problem." The smile disappeared. "They want to move into it pretty quick. They're gonna do the rest of the work with their own contractor."

"Not possible," Donny said, and turned back to the house.

Perry ran after him. I mean, he actually scampered,

like a big little kid. I hated Perry then. He didn't give a shit about how his selling the fucking Victorian, would impact me and Don or whether the work would be done the way it needed to be. I'm sure those things never even crossed his mind. "What do you mean, 'Not possible'? I told you they have money. Plenty of it." Perry tried a weak laugh.

Donny turned around to face him, adjusted his tool belt, like it was a gun belt. "What I mean, asshole, is that not just anybody can do the work on this place."

"Why not?" Perry asked. "It's just banging a few more boards into place, right?"

I saw Donny's right shoulder drop and pull back. I waited for what would come next. Perry could never understand what that old house meant to Don. How he'd studied the history of the place, pored over the old drawings, made sure every detail, every piece of trim, was authentic to the time period and done, whenever possible, with the tools the original builders would have used. I knew the idea of some rough carpenters using nail guns and paint sprayers, then designers making it a show place for rich assholes who would live in it for two weeks a year, made Donny go way dark. That house had become his friend and his patient. Don didn't like people, but he sure as hell loved that house—every hidden nook and cedar closet. It was a part of him. "Get the fuck out of here," is all Donny said then. And Perry was at least smart enough to know that it was time for him to move along. But before he did, as he walked back to his car, he called out to us. "They want to close the deal in two weeks. You guys will have to be gone by then."

Don didn't have much to say after Perry left, and it surprised me that he went right back to working on fitting trim pieces on the glass-fronted cabinets he'd built, each piece cut and beveled perfectly. "Measure twice, cut once," Donny had told me more than a few times. I kept working on the wainscoting, cutting the lumber we'd salvaged from the original kitchen on the table saw. "So what are we gonna do now?" I finally asked.

"I'm not doing anything." He stopped to light a cigarette, an unfiltered Camel. "Not till we're finished."

"What about Perry?"

"Fuck that prick."

"Yeah, man, but he owns the place."

Don stopped then and turned toward where I knelt, fitting a board into place. He looked haggard, eyes dark and baggy, hairline already deeply receded. I had no idea how old he was. In his forties, I guessed, though later found out he had been only thirty-two at the time. "Just keep working, Buddy. That's all we've got."

I didn't agree but wasn't about to argue. I was thinking about my own plans. What would I do next? Where could I go? Would Sully go with me? "Okay, man, whatever you say." I measured out the next board, marked it, and turned on the table saw. I'd learned to like the noise of construction; it drowned out all the crap in my head. We passed the rest of the day in our joint labor. And when we finished up Donny asked me if I wanted to fix. Told me he'd copped some black tar. "Good shit," he said.

"Can't do it, man. Think I'm done with all that."

"Yeah, since when?"

"It's fucking me up. Sully wants me to get clean."

"Pussy-whipped."

"Yeah, could be. I wouldn't call it that, though. I want to feel better is all."

"Your loss," Donny said as he put away his tools, each in its own place on the work bench and in his toolbox. When all that was done, he turned back to me. "What are you waiting for? Get the fuck out of here. Go play with your college pal."

"He's not my pal. We just went to school together. Perry's a dick."

"And what's that make you?"

"Hey, man," I said. "I know you're disappointed about the house and all, but don't take it out on me."

"What makes you think I give a shit about this fucking house?" He picked up a cut-off end of a 2x4 and held it in his hand. "Fuck this and fuck you all." He hurled the piece of lumber full force into the glass-fronted cabinet he'd spent the whole afternoon working on. It shattered into a hundred pieces. I had to duck away. He grabbed a framing hammer then and started smashing every other cabinet in the room.

I stood there watching. Maybe I even enjoyed what was happening. Maybe I even wanted to join in. But I didn't. After a few minutes, when most everything in that kitchen had been destroyed and Donny looked like he was wearing down, I came up behind him and grabbed him around the chest, pinning his arms against his side. "It's over, man. That's enough," I said quietly. "Let's go get high."

That was the last time for me. I woke up with a piercing headache and a growing cyst on the inside crook of my arm. Probably from the needle we shared. We didn't have the luxury then of clean works. I'd pay the price for that carelessness later in life. When I showed up at Sully's place, she took one look at me and brought me to the local doc. With both of them looking on, he drained the cyst. It was disgusting and cleansing at once. I felt deep shame, both for myself and for this woman (who I was beginning to love) to see me like this. I wasn't surprised when later that evening she told me we needed to "wrap it up."

"Yeah, I know," is all I said.

"I like you, Robert," she said. "But you've got a bunch

of stuff to figure out. I can't go there with you. Maybe some other time, some other life."

I stepped into her arms for one last hug. I never wanted to let go, but Sully finally pushed away. "Go on, now," she whispered. And I left.

I holed up in my room for the next week, shaking, crying, sweating; till I felt strong enough to walk on over to Perry's apartment and demand all my back pay, which I used to buy a beat-up old Dodge pick-up, and headed out of town the next day. I didn't even stop to say good-bye to Donny, though I wish to hell I had.

A few years later Perry called to say that Don had died. Not from an overdose as I'd expected, but from a liver cancer too far progressed to do anything about. He was only 39 years old when he went. I told Perry that I'd fly in from Seattle, where I live now with my wife and daughter, for the funeral.

"There's not going to be one," he said. "The guy didn't have any family that anybody knew of, so we just went ahead and cremated him. I paid for it, five hundred fucking dollars."

I stared at the phone in my hand, unable to put a name to what I was feeling. "When did it happen?"

"About a week ago. He was in the hospital for only a

day or two, but he was already too far gone. Skin was all yellow, and he looked like he'd swallowed a basketball. Not something you wanta see, Buddy."

"How'd you find out?"

"I guess Donny had my name written down in his wallet, so the hospital called me. Pretty sad, to die like that. All alone."

I didn't think Perry sounded very sad. I didn't want to talk to him anymore. "Okay then. Thanks for letting me know."

"Sure, no problem. You were probably the only friend the guy ever had."

"No, I wasn't, man. I left. And never looked back. That's not much of a friend, is it?" I wasn't really asking for an answer. And didn't get one.

"You should come visit sometime," Perry said. "You wouldn't believe how much this place has changed."

"Yeah, I'll do that," I told him and hung up the phone.

I stared out the window that looked out over Lake Union for a long time until my wife, Meg, came up behind me. "What's wrong, honey?" she asked.

And so I told her. About Donny. About how we worked together. About the junk (though she already knew about that part of my life). And about how lost I'd felt back then. "He was a decent guy," I said. "And a damn good carpenter. I wish I could have been there for him."

"You loved him, didn't you?" Meg touched my arm.

"I don't know. Maybe." I tried to stop from crying, but I couldn't.

Boys Will Be Boys

It happened at the Jersey Shore, Long Beach Island to be exact. My dumbass cousin Barry and I were going to the *Lifeguard's Ball.* Don't ask me why. It's not like we had dates or anything. And I wasn't even a lifeguard. Barry was, even though we were both only sixteen, too young for the job. But Barry was already shaving and had hair on his chest, so had been able to convince Louie Grazon, the lifeguard captain, that he was 18.

The *Lifeguard's Ball* happened at the end of every summer and was kind of a big deal. All the guards wore jackets and ties, and their dates wore sparkly dresses. "There's all kind of good-looking chicks there," Barry said. "Maybe you'll even score." Then he laughed. Barry knew that I was still a virgin. He claimed that he'd been with lots of girls. I didn't know whether to believe him. Barry was always bragging. I don't know why I kept hanging out with him. All he ever did was try to put me down. Still, there was something about him that made me keep coming back for more. Maybe I just needed someone to talk to. The world was still a puzzle to me, and Barry seemed to have the answers. At least he acted like he did.

The first thing Barry did when we got to the L.B.I. Community Center, where the big dance was being held, was pull out a pint of cheap whiskey that he had stolen from his father's liquor cabinet. He took a sip, then offered the bottle to me. I shook my head. I didn't like the taste of hard liquor, and I was already feeling very uncomfortable, looking around at all the handsome, muscular lifeguards and their fancied-up dates. I wanted to get out of there. "Come on, Buddy," Barry said. "Don't be such a pussy." So, yeah, I took a nip then. It burned going down. "There you go," Barry said. "I'll make a man of you yet."

"Eat shit," I told him. I felt totally out of place. I quickly scoped out the most secluded corner to hide in while I watched Barry as he darted around the dance floor, poking his fat head into one group after another. Knowing my jerk-off cousin, I knew he was making what my mom would call "inappropriate comments" to all the girls. The other lifeguards glared at him, but Barry didn't seem to notice.

Every once in a while, Barry would remember that I was there, and saunter over to my corner. "Get out and circulate, little man. Do some dancing; show us those Philly moves."

"I don't see you dancing, hotshot."

"Barry doesn't dance. Barry is a lover, not a dancer."

"Why don't we get out of here?" I said. "There aren't any single girls anyway."

"That's what you think."

"We don't belong here. I'm leaving."

That's when Captain Louie saw us, sauntered over and pointed at me. "What's he doing here? Lifeguards and their dates only." Louie was a big guy with huge shoulders that threatened to tear his suit jacket open. But I didn't feel scared of him. Maybe it was the whiskey.

I looked him right in the eye and said, "Guess I'm Barry's date then."

Louie snorted a laugh. "Yeah, you look like his type."

Barry pushed me in the chest. "Shut up, punk."

I pushed him back. Hard. And before I knew what was happening, Barry and I were swinging away at each other. Louie didn't even try to stop us. A crowd gathered around. I could hear them laughing and cheering. Barry outweighed me by 40 pounds, but I was holding my own, I thought. I even got in a solid right to my cousin's nose and was pleased to see blood spurt out.

"That's enough," Louie finally said and grabbed us both up by our arms. "Party's over. You two assholes get the fuck out of here. Now!" He pushed us roughly toward the door.

We sidled out of the room, as the rest of the guards chuckled and went back to their dancing.

Outside, I looked at Barry as he held a handkerchief up to his bloody nose. "You were right," I said. "That was fun."

"Your cousin Barry is a barbarian," my mother said the next morning when I told her what happened. "You should keep your distance from him."

"He's not so bad," I said. "Anyway, he's my cousin."

"Second cousin. I've never liked that side of the family."

"Still, he's my friend."

Mom put a plate of fried eggs in front of me. "Friends don't treat each other like that."

I would have argued more, but I knew she was right. And over the rest of that summer, I spent less and less time with my (second) cousin. I even found some new friends to hang out with. Nice guys (and one girl) who were into surfing. We'd spend hours riding waves and kidding around, sometimes playing touch football on the beach. Barry told me he thought surfing was for pussies. I told him that didn't make any sense, and walked away before he could say anything else. When I found out the next summer that Barry and his family would not be coming down the shore that year, it didn't bother me at all.

Crybaby

I wasn't surprised when my older sister called to tell me that our mother was dying and that she probably wouldn't make it through the night, and that I should get back there as soon as possible. I wasn't surprised, but I was shocked and started crying. My sister, Hannah, said, "Don't start crying."

"I can't help it," I told her.

"Well, we're the ones who have to deal with this. And none of us are crying. You have to be strong, Buddy."

"I'll call you back," was all I could manage before I hung up and really gave myself over to sobbing. My mother was eighty-eight years old and wasn't going to make it to eighty-nine, but that wasn't why I was crying. I was crying for myself. When my father died thirteen years earlier, I didn't cry at all. And I was right there when it happened, holding his hand, stroking his forehead, listening to the rattle in his chest and the awful wheezing. When he was gone, I went out to the living room to tell my mother, who was sitting there waiting, wringing her hands. I guess she couldn't bring herself to watch him die. I said, "Dad's gone now." And before I could form another sentence, I started choking up and couldn't get the words out. My mother looked at me and said, "Don't you start that. Or else I will too." And that was the end of it. That's the way we are in my family.

I started calling the airlines to see about getting a ticket home right away. Maybe I could even get there before Mom died. But when I told the airline people what my situation was, I found out that since my mother was still alive, they would have to charge me full fare, which without an advance reservation was almost two thousand dollars. If she were already dead, then they could give me the bereavement fare, which was only three hundred bucks. I didn't want to lie about my mother's impending death. On the other hand, I didn't have two grand for an airline ticket to the East Coast. So, I told the next airline I called that I wanted the bereavement special. I should have figured, they weren't going to say, sure, no problem, Buddy, sorry for your loss. They wanted to know who the funeral director was and what was his phone number. I told them that Mom had just died and was still in the hospital. Then they wanted to know, which hospital and which doctor. Since I had that information, I gave it to them, and they made the reservation for me right then without checking. By this time, my tears were gone.

When I finally got into Philadelphia and made my way out to the hospital, Mom was already gone. My brother and sister took me into the room where Mom was lying on the hospital bed staring up at the ceiling. Well, I guess she wasn't really staring, but that's what it looked like. They hadn't even pulled a sheet over her or anything. I immediately fell apart again and sat down in the chair beside Mom's bed and took hold of her hand and started crying. My brother and sister scurried out of the room. After a while I got thirsty and took a drink from the water glass that was on the bedside table. Damn, I thought, that was the same water my mother drank from before she died. I sucked it up right through the same hospital glass straw. I was sitting there holding Mom's hand and staring at the water glass when Hannah and Steve came back in the room. "What are you doing?" Hannah said.

"Nothing. What am I supposed to be doing?" I put the water glass down.

"Look, we have to get moving now," my brother said. "There are things to do."

"What do you mean?"

"Arrangements have to be made."

"Oh yeah, right," I said. "I didn't think it happened so fast."

My sister walked over to stand behind me and put her hand on my shoulder, which was pretty strange. People in my family aren't touchers—certainly not in any way that might be interpreted as intimate. "The nurses," she said, and squeezed my shoulder.

"What about them?"

"They were very good to Mom. They seemed to like her."

"Yeah?"

"That's all I wanted to say. But I think you need to let go of her hand now."

"She's got to be moved," Steve said. "We've all been waiting for you."

"Right now?"

"They need the room."

"I don't understand," I said. "I just got here. "

"We'll go get something to eat," Hannah said. "You must be hungry."

We went to the Melrose Diner. It's where we always went to eat when I was in town. The food isn't all that good, but it is comfortable in a way. "Are you hungry?" Steve asked me.

"No, not really, but I can eat."

"You can always eat," Hannah said.

"I'm going to have a corned beef sandwich," I said.

"The corned beef is good here," Steve said.

"What are you going to have?"

"The turkey chili," he said. "They give you a lot. Last time I couldn't even finish it all."

"You can take what's left home with you," Hannah told him. "Have it for lunch tomorrow."

"That's what I was thinking," he said. Steve lives

alone, a bachelor all his life. I worry that he's lonely, but don't ever ask him about it. Don't think he'd have much to say if I did.

Hannah ordered vegetable soup and a roll. She was on a vegetarian diet, she said. She also said she'd lost almost eleven pounds.

I said, "You have good willpower."

"Anybody can do it. You just have to have discipline."

"What about dessert?"

"What about it?"

"I always like to have dessert with my dinner. That's why I never lose any weight."

"You look skinny," Hannah said.

"Yeah, I guess." I took a sip of my iced tea. "Do you remember the cake plate?"

"What cake plate?" Steve asked.

"Mom's cake plate. When we were kids if you ate all your dinner, Mom would bring out the cake plate. Remember?"

"Not really," Hannah said. Steve shook his head.

"Oh come on, you've got to remember that. It was like aluminum or steel or something, with a big glass plate under it."

"It couldn't have been steel," Steve said. "Nobody would use steel for a cake plate."

"Okay, so it wasn't steel. I'm talking about Mom. About when we were kids."

"Even aluminum seems unlikely," Steve said. "It was probably plastic."

"It wasn't plastic," I shouted. "It was fucking aluminum."

"You're making a scene," Hannah said.

Later we had to go to the funeral home and pick out a coffin. It felt like we were buying a new car. Did we want the one with the chrome or the one made of mahogany that would "last forever"? "Why does it need to last forever?" I asked, but nobody answered. Off in a corner, I saw a plain wooden box and wandered over to look at it. "How much is this one?" I shouted over to the director guy who was showing one of the Cadillac coffins to Steve and Hannah. They all looked up at me and my sister made one of those faces like she just bit into something sour.

"You don't want that one," the director said.

"Why not? It looks like it would do the job. It even has a Mogen David carved on it. I like it."

"That's for the Orthodox," the director said, "It wouldn't be right for your mother. It would make the family look needy."

I was ready to start arguing with him, partly inspired by the growing realization of how much this whole deal was going to cost. I wanted to be outraged but couldn't quite pull it off. We ended up going for the middle-of-the-road coffin with the satin bed liner. I could have gone to Spain for six months and sat on the beach for what it cost, but I guess that's no way to think about the expense of your mother's funeral. The coffin was only the beginning. We also had to pay to rent the space and hire the Rabbi and even get a bunch of finger food. It was like we were throwing a party. At least the director was arranging everything. Dying is pretty complicated when you get right down to it.

All of this was happening very fast. When someone dies, especially when you're Jewish, you don't get to take your time. You're supposed to get the loved one in the ground within 24 hours. That's the Jewish law, which probably made sense back in the old days, before refrigeration. We pushed on and scheduled the funeral for the next day, which was actually longer than the 24 hours, but we got a special dispensation from the director who said he was in contact with the Rabbi so everything was kosher. What I was noticing as we made all these preparations and called all the relatives, was that neither my brother or sister seemed all that upset that our mother was dead. In fact, neither of them had said one word about her. It was like we were purposely avoiding what was the main focus of all our activities. I couldn't figure it out. Mom had been on her way out for a long time. In the last few years, she was a burden to everyone around her. All she did was complain and try to make the rest of the family feel guilty that they couldn't help her. My mother was a hard woman, no doubt about that. When she was younger and healthier, she was a tyrant. When she was old and sick, she was a pain in the ass.

I feel like I've got to say something to somebody that will get a response. I pick on my sister. She's the oldest and most like my mother in temperament. I'm not saying she's mean, not exactly. She's reserved and, I think, unhappy. But what do I know? I moved away a long time ago. We are sitting in the living room of her house in Cherry Hill, New Jersey. The heavy curtains are pulled closed across all the windows and the house is dark except for the light from the massive television that takes up one corner of the room. My brother-in-law, Sidney, is watching a football game. The TV is so big, the players look life-size, like they're going to burst out of the screen. I know Sidney has money riding on this game and a bunch of other ones, so he's pretty serious about the whole deal and not interested in talking to me. I don't follow sports anymore, so there's not much I can contribute to the football watching. I say shit like, "They're in trouble now," or "You gotta throw on third down." Sidney ignores me. Anyway, it's Hannah who I'm after. When she gets up from the couch and goes into the kitchen I get up and follow her.

"So how are you doing with all this?" I ask.

"Don't start, Buddy. I'm not in the mood."

"I'm not starting."

"Yes you are. You've been waiting all day to start with me. I know you."

'No, you don't. You just think you do."

"I know you weren't here for the last thirteen years. I know that Steve and I were the ones who were with Mom every day. Taking her to the doctors, trying to get her to eat, changing her."

"Changing her?"

"For the last two years she was having accidents. She wouldn't admit she was incontinent. Steve was doing her shitty laundry every day."

"Why didn't you tell me?"

"What good would it have done? Were you going to come back and help out?"

"We could have put her in a facility, in a—what do you call it—an extended care thing. I told you all along I'd be willing to help pay."

"Pay, schmay. What were we supposed to do? Drag her there? She said she'd rather die than go to one of those places."

"That's what all old people say. She would have adjusted."

"You couldn't make Mom do anything. Didn't you understand that?"

"I guess everybody understands what they want to understand."

"That's for sure."

"Look, I don't want to fight with you, Hannah. And, yes, I really appreciate everything you and Steve did for Mom. She was a challenging woman."

"You don't know the half of it."

I sit down at the kitchen table. Hannah is fussing about, slicing cheese and salami to put on Ritz Crackers to bring to Sidney. She doesn't offer me any. I start scratching out some ideas on a notebook I carry with me. I know it will get her attention.

"What are you writing there?"

"Just some notes."

"Notes for what?"

"About Mom. Someone has to deliver the eulogy."

She doesn't say anything. Stews around for a few minutes, takes Sidney his snack, then comes back and sits across from me at the table. I keep scribbling.

"This isn't right," she finally says.

"What isn't?"

"What you're doing."

"What am I doing?"

"Trying to take over. It's what you always do when you come back."

"That's not true." I think about it. "Is it?"

"I'm the oldest. I'm the one who should speak."

"Well, what were you planning to say?"

"I wasn't. Not till you started in."

"Look, Hannah, I'm confused. If you weren't going to say anything, why do you care if I do?"

"Because you'll say something stupid. I know you, Buddy. You'll embarrass us all."

"Thanks a lot."

"It's not your place."

"Fine. Then you do it."

"No."

"Jesus, you're driving me crazy here. I'll tell you what. Why don't we do it together? We'll get Steve to help too."

"Steve doesn't have anything to say."

"How do you know that?"

"I just know. He's my brother."

"And what am I?"

"You're different."

I put my ballpoint pen down and stand up. Suddenly I feel very tired. "So, you don't even want to hear what I've been writing?"

"Maybe we should just let the Rabbi handle the eulogy."

"The Rabbi never even knew Mom. What's he going to say?"

"We'll talk to him. They know how to do these things. It'll be easier."

"Not for me it won't."

"Okay already. Tell me what you want to say. But don't make a big deal, okay?"

"What's wrong with making a big deal? Your mother only dies once."

She shakes her head. "Just read it, Buddy, okay?"

"It's not something I can just read. It's more extemporaneous."

"Extemporaneous?"

"Yeah, like off the cuff, impromptu."

"I know what the word means."

"Then why'd you ask me?"

"Just read it, dammit."

"Don't get angry with me."

"Read, already."

"Okay, but I'm not reading. These are just notes." I pause while Hannah settles back into the chair. I can tell by the look on her face, a combination of a scowl and a smirk, that whatever I say now will be greeted with hostility. I press on. "So, Esther Foreman, our mother. She tried to be a good mother I think, but in her final years nobody liked her very much. Not even herself."

"Stop! Stop right there, Buddy." Hannah pushes away from the table and stands up. "This is what I mean. 'Nobody liked her very much'? That's what you want to say at our mother's funeral?"

"Well, it's true."

"That's not the point. You say nice things in a eulogy. That's what the word means—to eulogize."

"It can mean other things." I check my notes and look up at her. She's still frowning. "Okay, I'll skip that part. Sit down, please."

"I don't like this, Buddy. Not one bit."

"I promise I won't say anything offensive, okay? I'm just trying to be real."

She sits down and makes a cheese cracker for herself. "Do what you want. I don't have the energy to argue."

"Good. Don't worry. I'll be careful."

"I'm going to bed." She stands up, no longer interested in my eulogy notes. "I'll see you in the morning."

"How about a hug?" I say. "I think I need it."

"Yeah," she says. "Maybe I do too." I hug my sister. She's stiff and only holds on a minute before she pushes me away. "Just don't say crazy stuff tomorrow, okay?"

"Goodnight, Hannah."

"Goodnight." I feel a twinge of affection for her as she walks away. She's my sister and I know her life hasn't been easy. I go and join Sidney on the couch to watch football.

◊ ◊ ◊

There are all kinds of people at the funeral. I'm surprised. I didn't think my mother had many friends left alive. But the old people and the extended family show up at the funeral home, dressed in black. I didn't bring a suit. I borrowed a jacket and tie from my brother that don't fit at all well and that make me feel like I just stepped out of a movie about the seventies. Hannah, Sidney, Steve, and I are in the front row. Everyone who comes in does this little sorry dance down the line of us. "Such a tragedy." "She was a good person, your mother." "A *shonda*." I don't know what to say, so I space out, paste a grim smile on.

When everyone is seated and some Jewish prayers are recited, the rent-a-Rabbi does his thing. He talks about my mother like she was some kind of saint, the best person to ever live on the planet. I'm guessing my sister filled his head with these untruths, but everyone around me is nodding and some are even crying. I feel like crying too. I want to mourn for the fictive woman he is talking about.

Then it's my turn. I hurry up to the podium, look out at all the mourners. They look back at me, sizing me up, expecting more of the same, I guess. I am suddenly nervous. Hannah was right. I've got no right to be doing this. "My mother, Esther, was not an easy woman. No way. I'm not sure what the Rabbi was talking about—that wasn't the Esther Forman I knew." I look out at the crowd again. They appear puzzled, and a bit more interested. Hannah is looking down at her lap. "I guess Mom tried her best. She made me take piano lessons, even though I didn't want to. And as soon as I was able to, I quit and never played again. To this day, I can't even stand to listen to people play piano. I guess my point here is that sometimes people do what they think is best for their families, but what they are really doing is for themselves. Know what I mean?" Now when I look out, the audience seems confused, but even more attentive. "Yesterday my sister told me that I had ignored my mother for the last 13 years of her life. I have to admit this is true. I did that and I'm ashamed of it, but I did it because I had to save myself. That's how it goes sometimes. Mom wanted to control me. Or she wanted to fight with me. She did that to Hannah and Steve too, but they stuck around and took it. God bless them. Someone had to—especially after my father died. But it wasn't going to be me. I moved out to the West Coast to get away from her. I know that's not the way a son should treat his mother. That's what I did though, and, to tell you the truth, I think it saved my life. I'm sorry, Mom." I stop then and try to catch my breath. People have their mouths open now. Hannah looks like she is about to explode, though I notice too that Steve has a half-smile on his face. "I think the people who were around her at the end are not too disappointed that my mother has died. I know that sounds harsh, but what are you going to do? Although I will say—and my sister told me this—that the nurses at the hospital seemed to like Mom pretty well. So that's a good thing. And, despite everything, I will miss her. In her own way, she loved us all. She was my mother and, for better or worse, I am her son. And I guess that's all I have to say." I shrug and walk back to my seat.

I don't remember a whole lot about the rest of the service, not even much about the burial. I know I dropped a handful of dirt and pebbles on to the coffin after the cemetery workers lowered it into the grave. I remember the sound of those pebbles bouncing off the metal. It was like I was throwing dirt on my mother. For a second, I thought she was going to get up and start yelling at me. I'd had enough. I knew then it was time for me to go home. Maybe then I would cry some more and think about the life my mother had lived.

Injuries

We were all scared of my father. With good reason. He was an angry man. I knew that even before I knew there were different types of people, both good and bad, kind and not so. Dad was mostly silent but given to sudden outbursts of fury. You never knew when he might explode or what might set him off. I once stood behind his easy chair, the one that only he was allowed to sit in, and in my youthful playfulness tapped on the bald spot at the back of his head. It was a foolish thing to do, and Dad responded in a way I should have expected. He sprang up from the chair, turned around and pushed me to the ground, then stood staring down at me. I scrambled up and ran crying from the room as he settled back into the big chair.

So, I was surprised when one day Dad arrived home from his office carrying a small brown-paper bag and proceeded to call all three of us kids together in the living room. We looked at each other in confusion, probably expecting the worst. I considered making a run for it. Maybe I could hide in my room and lock the door.

But then Dad opened that grease-stained bag and showed us what was inside. He pulled out four small sugar cones, topped with marshmallow and chocolate sprinkles. They were the most amazing treats I'd ever seen at the time—a seven-year-old's greatest fantasy. I didn't understand then what possessed him to make such a gesture. All I knew was that I wanted that candy cone more than I'd ever wanted anything in my young life. I'm sure my sister and younger brother felt the same. It felt like we were all vibrating with desire.

Dad said, still holding the cones, "Since there are four cones and only three of you, whoever finishes first, gets to have the extra one." I think he smiled then; it was strange to see. He then handed each of us a cone, with the warning, "Don't start eating till I tell you to."

There we each stood, staring at the sweet treats in our hands. I was raring to go, determined to win that extra cone. I glanced to my left, where my wimpy older sister Hannah stood. She had a puzzled look on her face. I knew I could beat her. She probably wouldn't even try. Then I turned to my right where my younger brother Steve was. I wasn't sure about him; he was a pretty quiet kid. But when Dad finally barked, "Okay, go!" I jammed that cone into my mouth as fast as I possibly could, barely chewing or tasting and swallowed it down in three furious bites. "I win!" I shouted. "I win."

"Yep. You won alright," Dad said, and handed me my prize, that fourth cone. I looked over at my sister then. She was only half-way through her cone, a dreamy smile on her face. Steve was taking little bites out of his; he still had almost all his cone left.

It was then that I felt a painful knot in my stomach, like everything in there was red and twisted. I bent over in agony, thinking I might have to rush to the bathroom. I wanted to cry but knew Dad would not stand for that. I stood up, still holding my prize, and stared at my father. "You happy now?" he asked. It wasn't a question that needed an answer.

Fair to say, I've struggled all my life with my relationship with my father. I'm not sure I can even call it a relationship— a competition maybe, a searching? For what, I'm not sure. I'd early on given up on affection—that I knew was out of the question. I would have settled for recognition. Like, "Hi kid, how you doing?" But Dad was too dignified for that, too stoic, too withdrawn. Our communication was so limited, I never knew what he thought. As a child, all I could figure was that he was almost always mad at me. He stomped around the house, looking like he'd just received some very bad news. I couldn't help thinking that news was about me.

Dad was a general practitioner, the neighborhood doc. He had his office on the first floor of our house, so we were always aware of his business, the patients coming and going would trigger a buzzer in the front door. And when my brother and I left the house, to go play in the park, we would walk by his waiting room filled with anxious patients. It made me proud that Dad was such an important person in the neighborhood, but it also made him even more unapproachable. I mean, who was I to expect attention from such a man. He was too busy for the likes of me. He had sick people to attend to, people with serious problems.

Then it came to me. If I wanted my father's attention, I would have to get sick or injured myself. Then Dad would have to see me, even touch me, like one of his patients.

It started with scrapes and bruises. I became purposely reckless: tipping over my soap-box scooter while zipping down the steep hill on Larchwood avenue, sliding into second base on the sandlot field while wearing short pants (my leg got scraped up good on that one) or getting into fights with kids who were way bigger than me (Richie Sabo busted my nose when I called him a chickenshit). Then I'd go running into my father's office—making sure that he wasn't with a patient—and display my wounds, grimacing appropriately and, of course, holding back any tears. Feelings were not a good way to get Dad's attention or approval. Happy, sad, or pained; keep it to yourself, be a man.

But Dad always responded well when I came to him. He tended my wounds—tender being the correct word. "That's a nasty one," he'd say, almost smiling as he sprayed the wound with stinging disinfectant. "You must have been running really fast."

"Yeah, I guess, I beat all the kids down the hill, even Joey Klein."

"You're a tough kid, Buddy," he said, as he applied more bandages than were probably necessary. He was a different man then, both my father and my healer. He was the Dad I really wanted but could only have in these brief moments of blood.

Now I was hooked. And the injuries continued: twisted ankles, broken bones, bleeding wounds—those were all good. Worthy of Dad's attentions and ministrations. It was then I got to tell him some long, imagined adventure about sliding into home plate to win the game for my team, but, in the process, receiving a deep purple bruise on my right leg. Dad would nod and continue to bandage or disinfect, one time administering stitches—without pain killers of any sort other than my own desire to please.

I treasured these moments with my father, the laying on of hands. In memory, I still do. They were my only chance to connect. Dad hardly spoke at home. Even dinners were silent affairs. As Mom warned us, "Don't bother your father. He needs to relax." Strong and silent, Dad was. A Jewish John Wayne. I longed for his approval. But as time went by, the harder I tried, the more distant he became, even when I thought I was doing exactly what he wanted me to do—and be. After a time, even the injuries couldn't hold his attention, and eventually he accused me of faking them. Then I did cry—but only after I left his office.

By the time I got to junior high school, I had given up on trying to get Dad to be a real father to me. I wasn't sure what that would look like. My models of fatherhood were limited. I didn't want a television dad, like Ward Cleaver or the *Bonanza* dad. I knew that was bullshit. None of my friends had fathers like that—sympathetic and fair. All my friends had messed-up relationships with their fathers too. I mean, some of them were getting regularly beat on. Dad only hit me a few times. When I was fifteen, I swung back at him. He didn't hit me again after that. But he didn't talk to me either.

But for all the storm and disappointment of our relationship, I still did love my father; it was baked in. And I believe, in his own tortured way, he loved me too. He just couldn't show it. And after a while, neither could I. By the time I was about to leave for college, a deep chasm had opened between us. I was convinced that my father was deeply disappointed with me. Most of this was conveyed to me by my mother. "You're breaking your father's heart. You know that, don't you?" she asked, hovering over me as I packed my one suitcase. "He expected more from you. We all did."

"More what?" I threw my underwear into the suitcase. "I'm going to college, aren't I? Being a good boy."

"This isn't how we wanted you to do it. You could have gone to Penn. A full scholarship—and he turns it down? What kind of son does this?"

"Mom, who're you talking to? It's just us here."

"Don't be fresh. You know what I'm talking about. You tell me, Buddy, just so I know. Why do you decide to go to this little college that nobody's ever even heard of and turn down a scholarship?"

"Stop with the scholarship already. We don't even need it. Dad makes plenty of money."

"Don't tell me how much money your father makes. This is none of your business."

I placed my transistor radio in the case and slammed it shut. "What's done is done. I'm sorry if I've disappointed you and Dad. That wasn't my intention."

She softened a little then. "At least you'll be taking the pre-med classes."

"Right, pre-med," I agreed, though I had no intention of doing anything of the sort. I didn't want to become a doctor like my father, though I well understood that was the expectation. "I've already signed up for Anatomy 101."

"I'll tell your father," Mom said. "He'll be pleased."

"Right," I said. "I know." I smiled at my mother as she left my bedroom. I couldn't wait to get out of there. That's why I had turned down the scholarship to the University of Pennsylvania. No way was I going to spend one more day living at home. Marion College would do just fine; five hundred miles between me and my family. And there I could finally be myself. Whoever that was.

Before I left though, I felt the need to talk to my father one last time. I didn't know what I expected, only that I wanted to fill a gap. I was hoping he would say something I could take with me, something that would sooth the pain I was feeling, like he had done when I came to him with my childhood wounds. And, like before, I approached him in his office. He sat behind his wide oak desk, puffing on a pipe. "Could we talk for a minute?" I asked.

He motioned for me to sit down in the chair opposite him, though he continued to look at a medical journal he had open in front of him.

"So, I'm going off to college," I stuttered. "Bobby Fisher's dad is going to drive us to the Greyhound station."

Dad nodded. And waited for me to go on. I couldn't read him at all. Thought about leaving but decided to make one last grasp for connection. "You know, I don't hate you," I said, the words splashing out seemingly beyond my control. "But I don't understand why it's always so hard with you. I mean, you won't even talk to me, Dad."

He put the pipe down and closed the magazine. "What the hell are you talking about, boy?"

"You know that's true, don't you? I don't even know if you like me. And I can't go off to school wondering about that."

Dad stared at me for what seemed a long time before he spoke. "I've done the best I could with you. Given you everything that you need—a nice house, your own bedroom, good food and clothing. You've never appreciated any of it. You're a selfish kid, Buddy. That's all there is to it. Maybe when you get to college you'll grow up a little and stop all this whining."

"That's what this is to you?" I sat upright in the hard-wooden chair. "I'm just fucking whining?"

"You watch your damn mouth."

I could feel the room grow small, constricted by our mutual anger. I could barely see, tried to speak, but Dad stood up, pushed away from his desk. His face was red and contorted. "Get out of my office. Now. And don't come back till you learn some respect."

"Fine!" I stood and took a step around the desk, moving toward him, not knowing what I would do, till we were only inches apart. I realized only then that I was now taller than my father. I could smell his tobacco breath. He took a step back. Then turned away. I raised my hand, formed a fist. "Look at me!" I yelled.

Dad turned back. "Are you going to hit me, Buddy? Go ahead. See what happens."

Every muscle in my body tensed. I pulled back my arm, stared hard at this man who was my father. Waited. Then stopped, felt something shift inside of me, like a heavy padlock snapping shut. My fist and all my dark fury dropped away and I was left only with a deep sadness and a strange sense of completion. “I’m done with this, Dad,” I said. “All done.” Without another word, I turned away and left that office. It would be years before I returned.

Don't Ever Forget Me

I stand there on the side of the highway with my thumb out, thinking, how the fuck did I get here? And it's cold, really cold. I'd realized a couple hours ago that I wasn't dressed for this weather, wearing my regular dumb-ass college boy outfit—jeans and a hooded sweatshirt with Marion College emblazoned across the front. I have a wool hat that I pull down over my ears.

I'm going home for the Christmas break; that's what they call it at school. My family is Jewish, but we don't even do Hanukkah seriously. When I was growing up sometimes there was a present or two for my brother and sister and I so we wouldn't feel so jealous of all the Christian kids with their new bikes and sweaters.

As I stand here shivering, I wonder why I'm even bothering. I don't much like being with my family and I know once again I'll feel like I'm a big disappointment to them because I decided to go to this oddball little school in the middle of Ohio when I could have gone to Penn— an

Ivy League school where both my father and sister were alumni—a fact they would no doubt remind me of.

Just then I see headlights coming toward me out of the evening mist—the first car I've seen in a while. I hold my thumb out high and put on my best version of a smile. This is my last chance for a ride, I figure. The car is coming on fast, and I see as it approaches that it's a green sports car with, surprisingly, the top down. My heart tom-toms as the little car screeches to a stop a few yards beyond where I am posed. I grab my backpack and race to catch up.

"Thanks, man," I say when I reach the car. A young guy is sitting behind the wheel— older than me, but not by much. He looks straight ahead, like I'm not there. And I think for a second that maybe this is all a bad dream.

But then he looks over at me and says, "You know how to drive?"

"Yeah, man. Definitely."

"Don't call me man." He stares at me, like he's deciding something. "Okay, get in then."

I toss my backpack behind the seat, climb in, and the guy guns the engine. I take a deep breath and smile at my good luck. "Nice car," I say.

"It's a TR-4, quick little bird."

"I'll bet," I say, even though I don't know anything about a TR-4.

He shifts to a higher gear and the car shoots ahead.

"I've been driving for 20 hours straight. I need a damn rest."

"Cool," I say. "My name's Buddy, by the way." There's no reciprocation.

A few miles later, he hits the brakes and we skid to a stop. "You're gonna drive now." He gets out and we switch places. My hands are shaking. I haven't told him that I don't know how to drive a stick.

I'm not about to give up this sweet ride though, so I settle in behind the wheel, adjust the seat, and the mirrors, stalling for time, and turn the key. The engine roars to life, like some kind of animal woken from sleep and ready for the hunt. I glance over at the owner. His head is nodding, eyes bleary. Looks like he's ready to fall asleep right then and there. That is if I don't drive his pretty car into the side of a cliff. "It's got five gears," he mumbles. "You probably won't need them all."

"Yeah, right," I say, looking down at the floor shifter and wondering how I'm gonna get myself out of this. I feel a moment of relief when I see that the shifter knob has a little diagram of where the gears are. I drive an old Vespa at school, one that I bought for fifty bucks from a townie kid. It barely runs, but it does have gears and a clutch, so I have some idea about the relationship between shifting and clutching. But the translation is far from clear. "Uh," I begin, trying to get his attention before he completely zonks out. "What's your name?" I'm not going to come right out and tell him I don't know how to drive his pretty little car.

"Does that matter?" he says. I note how he's like the perfect guy to be driving a sports car. A mop of dirty blonde hair, leather jacket, deep tan, long and lanky. I'd bet a million dollars he's in some elitist fraternity.

"Doesn't matter. Nope. Just wondering."

"It's Richard," he says. "Now, come on, let's get going."

I feel around with my feet, trying to distinguish the gas pedal from the brake and the clutch. I know they are all down there somewhere. I put my left hand on the wheel, the right nudging that stubby, beautiful, leather-topped gearshift, and for a moment I feel like I actually know what I'm doing, like maybe I own this damn car. "So, Rich, I start off in first, right?"

He looks over at me, like it's the first time he's really noticed me. "It's Richard, not Rich," he says.

"The clutch is the one on the left, isn't it?"

"What the hell." He sits up straight. "You don't know how to drive, do you?"

"Well, that's not exactly true." I think I should tell him about the Vespa but decide against it. "It's just really cold, you know. Could we put the top up? It's gonna be dark soon."

"We can do that later. So just drive if you know how. Let's go, man."

"The name's Buddy." Two can play the name game. I push the clutch in and ease the shifter toward what I think is first gear. The damn thing won't budge. As cold as it is, I feel sweat begin to run down my back. I try pushing harder and a terrible grinding noise fills the air. "Stop!" Richard screams. "What the hell are you doing?"

"I forgot to push the clutch all the way in." Now I am sweating and shivering at once. I silently berate myself. What twenty-year-old doesn't know how to drive a damn stick-shift car? Somewhere in my fevered brain I think, this is all my father's fault. He should have taught me how to drive a stick. I almost decide I should just get out and wait for the next ride—if there is one. But instead I try once more to get going. This time I get the shifter into first, but when I hit the gas, the damn car jumps up like a bucking bronco, then stalls out. I know I am done for and throw up my hands. I reach for my backpack, ready to get out.

Richard shakes his head. "Okay," he says, rubbing his hand across his eyes. "Let's quit the bullshit, okay? You have no idea how to drive this vehicle, do you?"

"I do not," I admit. "I'm sorry. I just really needed a ride."

He looks disappointed. "So, here's what we're going to do."

"What?" I'm on edge, wondering if this is going to get physical. I am not in the mood for a fight.

"Guess I'm going to teach your dumb ass how to drive."

I was going to argue the point. I mean, I did know how

to drive an automatic, but decide to shut up. "Yeah, that sounds good," I say.

Richard turns out to be an okay guy. He had been a fraternity boy at one point, he told me later, but had given it up, dropped out of college, and now spent most of his time surfing. He'd been driving all day and night from where he lived in Santa Cruz, wherever that was. But out here on the side of the highway, what did any of those details really matter? The man was a good teacher. I'll give him that. After only about 20 minutes and a few more bucks and stalls, I get the hang of the whole shifting thing. "You just have to be gentle with it," Richard says. "This is a precision machine. You gotta stroke her."

I think that is a funny way to put it, but he's right. The car will not let the driver (me) jam it into some place it doesn't want to go. "Everything has to be smooth," Richard tells me. "Like riding a wave. Got it?"

"Yeah, I think so." I pat the leather steering wheel. "Go with the flow."

"Start off easy."

"We're not going to put the top up?"

"It doesn't work."

"When were you going to tell me that?"

"Drive," Richard says. So, I do.

Once I relax and let the car behave the way it is meant to, it's not that difficult. This vehicle, though, is like nothing

I've driven before. My father never lets me drive any of his new cars. I learned on my mother's clunky old Chevy station wagon. The only thing that station wagon and this Triumph have in common is that they both have license plates. I'm still freezing my ass off, but somehow I don't care now. I guess Richard feels I am doing okay, cause once I get it up to 60 and into the flow of the night, he slumps down in his seat and falls asleep. That's all he was bargaining for. I feel unreasonably proud of myself. The world suddenly is an okay place to be. It's been a long time since I felt this way. Maybe even since I was a kid, playing stickball in the street with Bruce Brown and Lizzie Stevenson, kids who lived on my block. All those old experiences are floating through my brain as I drive. I feel like I'm gliding, the car's doing the driving, I'm only there to keep an eye on it. At one point, though we're traveling through a curvy part of the road, lots of swinging left and right, I fall out of balance, out of synch with the TR-4 and the road underneath us. That's when Richard opens his eyes. I think he is going to start yelling or tell me what a dumbass I am, but instead he starts teaching again—all very calm and measured. "Here's how you handle the curves," he says. ""Give it a little brake going in, then accelerate slowly coming out. Just feel the momentum, Buddy."

I like that he calls me Buddy. And I handle the next curve like he said, and the one after that. "You got it," Richard says and closes his eyes again. I was hoping that he would stay awake and that maybe we could talk. I don't often get to talk to people—at least not seriously. I thought what a great time this would be to have a real conversation. So what if he's a spoiled, rich kid. Though I don't know if that's truly the case. I'm just judging by the fact that he has this car. For all I know, he stole the damn thing. "Hey, Richard," I hear myself saying. "You awake, man?"

"What is it?" Richard sits up and looks around. "Something wrong with the Triumph?" He rubs his eyes.

"No. The car's great. I've never driven anything like it. I'm not sure if I'm driving the car or it's driving me."

"Yeah, I know what you mean. That's kinda why I bought it."

"So, you did pay for it?"

"What's that supposed to mean?"

"Nothing, didn't mean to offend you. Just wondering, you know, how you could afford something like this. It had to be expensive, right?" I know I should shut up, but sometimes I can't help myself. Especially when I'm unsure of the situation. It's probably why I don't have a girlfriend. "I mean, how's a surfer afford this baby?"

"What the hell are you talking about?" He doesn't look angry, which maybe he should be. "I bought the car from a friend. I'm paying him a hundred bucks a month. Not that it's any of your business."

"Sorry. Sometimes I speak out of turn. My mom says I need to learn to filter myself."

"Don't worry about it," Richard says, then pauses. "Was there something else?"

"I'm not sure. It's just the road and all. It made me get to thinking."

"About what?"

"You know, like life and stuff."

"Life and stuff, huh? Pretty broad subject. Care to narrow it down a bit?"

"Well, like how do you live? I mean, like day to day. What keeps you going? What makes it worthwhile?"

Richard laughs. "Well, that really narrows it down."

"Sorry. Guess I'm feeling a little confused these days. I don't really know where I'm headed. Don't even know why the fuck I'm still going to college, or why I'm doing anything at all."

"Yeah, you're not going to learn any of that real shit in college." Richard reaches behind the seat and pulls out a heavy wool blanket and wraps it around his shoulders. "What you're wanting is an answer to an unanswerable question. Do you know what *existential* means?"

"Sort of," I say, wishing I had a blanket around my shoulders too. "I took a philosophy class when I was a freshman, but I don't remember much of it."

"It refers to the nature of existence and how none of

us measly humans know much of anything about why we're here, about our existence on the planet. I mean, we're all struggling. Every damn day."

"Isn't that what religion is for?"

"Shit. Religious people just pretend to have answers. You know why?"

"So they don't get scared?"

"Exactly." I feel better. Richard and I are talking. "But it's even worse than that. I mean, we're all scared, but religions take it a step further. For them to keep believing in their version of the big fairy tale, they have to make anybody who doesn't buy into that version wrong and bad. Next thing you know everybody's killing each other."

"That's pretty stark, man," I say. "Don't you believe in anything?"

"Just the waves."

"You believe in waves? Like waves in the ocean?"

"I do. Did you ever hear of a cat named Duke Kahanamoku?" He doesn't wait for an answer. "Well, he was one of the best surfers in Hawaii, a legend. You know what the Duke says?" Again, he doesn't wait for me to respond. "Be patient. Wave will come. Wave always comes." Richard looks over at me then like he's just revealed the secret of the universe.

He pulls the blanket tighter around his shoulders. "Everything I know about this life, I learned in the surf."

"Like how to not drown?"

"Is that a joke?"

"Sorry."

"Stop saying you're fucking sorry. It's a drag."

I almost say it again, a reflex. Instead, I blurt out, "Hey Richard, could we please stop someplace? Get a cup of coffee or something? I'm freezing my nuts off."

He laughs. "Much better response."

At the next exit, some anonymous town in Western Pennsylvania, I pull off and find a roadside cafe. Richard and I sit at the counter and order black coffee and pie. Blueberry for me, coconut custard for him. The pie's delicious, the best thing I've eaten in weeks, or maybe it's just that I'm so happy to be warm again. "I could do this for the rest of my life," I say out loud, though I hadn't meant to.

"Do what? Eat pie?"

"Something like that."

"You're a strange kid," Richard says.

"Seems to be the consensus opinion."

"I mean it in a good way." Richard gulps down the last of his coffee and holds his cup up for the waitress to see. "It's okay to be different. Easy as hell to be the same."

"I surf too, you know," I tell him.

"I thought you were from Philadelphia. Don't tell me they've got beaches in Philly."

"Nah, down the shore. In New Jersey. My family has a

little cottage on Long Beach Island. We go every summer. It's like my favorite place in the whole world."

"Well, I'm guessing you've got a lot more of the whole world left to see. But it's cool that you're a surfer. I wouldn't have guessed it."

"I'm not a real surfer. I kinda gave it up when I went off to college in middle-of-nowhere Ohio. I did love it, though. I body-surfed almost every day when I was a kid, then finally got myself a board when I graduated high school. My parents were not happy about me spending all that money on a surfboard when I was about to go off to college and they made this whole big deal about how I didn't have any idea of the value of money, which was bullshit since I'd had a damn job since I was thirteen."

"You need to come to California," Richard says. He's hardly eaten any of his pie. He gets up then and saunters over to the restroom.

I am tempted to eat what's left of his coconut custard. My blueberry pie is long gone. But I don't do that. I'm just saying I thought about it. But mostly my brain is seizing on that last word: California. I'd never been. Never been any farther west than Ohio. California seemed liked a different universe. Guys who grow up in Philadelphia mostly stay in Philadelphia. I'd never even heard of anyone who had gone as far away as California. My older sister had recently moved to New Jersey, but that was only like 20 miles away.

The only things I know about California are what I've seen on TV shows, like *77 Sunset Strip* and those Beach Blanket movies with Frankie Avalon and Annette Funicello, where they pretend to be surfers, but are clearly not. In fact, little Frankie is from South Philly and probably couldn't even lift a long board. I have a million questions ready for Richard when he comes back from the men's room, but he takes a last gulp of his coffee and says, "Let's hit it, brother. We've still got a long way to go."

Damn. I don't want to leave. I want to talk about California and surfing and how does someone just up and move to a place 3500 miles away from where he was born. "Aren't you going to finish your pie?" I ask.

"I'll drive now," Richard decides when we get outside. "All that caffeine has me stoked."

"Cool," I say, anticipating a chance to ask all my questions—and to claim the wool blanket, which I do as soon as I get in. Once we are back on the highway, I see how much better Richard drives the Triumph. He handles that little sports car like he's riding a long-breaking wave, shifting up and down to meet any condition, and going a hell of a lot faster than I would have dared. "A green car is hard to see at night," he tells me. "Cops don't bother you as much as if you had a red car. Red just makes them crazy. Of course, you have to be careful too."

"About the cops?"

"More about the truck drivers." He points ahead, where a big semi is huffing along. Richard drops down a gear and the car shoots ahead, pushing me back against the seat. "He probably can't see me coming up on him, so I have to do all the looking. Never know with truckers."

I was going to ask what you never know, but Richard guns it then and we are passing the big rig, flying by. In between gasps of air, I check out the speedometer. We're pushing 100. It's scary and thrilling all at once. I understand in that moment why a committed surfer would spend so much of his money on a fast car. As we pass the truck, I look up at the driver hunched over the wheel. Like Richard said, the guy doesn't look like he knew we were there at all. We slip back into the right lane and settle in, though still moving well past the 60-mph speed limit. I figure now would be a good time for more talk. I am thinking about how to get the conversation started when Richard nudges my shoulder and points. "Look up ahead. Another hitchhiker."

"Really? I don't see him." I squint, trying to pick him out of the blackness.

"Not a him," Richard says, and starts braking. "It's a girl."

I see her then, though it's hard to tell, from my viewpoint, whether it's a boy or a girl. But as we draw nearer and the headlights pick her up, I can see that Richard is right. It's a girl about my age, maybe older, with long hair, dressed in jeans and a pea coat, her thumb out, but not smiling. A suitcase alongside her. My first thought is that she must be freezing. As Richard pulls over, though, I say, "Where are we going to put her?" I'm suddenly afraid that Richard is going to put me out in favor of this more attractive hitcher.

"We can manage," he says. "You don't want to leave her out here, do you?"

"No, of course not," I answer quickly. "But there's only two seats."

"There's the crawl space behind us. And a trunk too. The British call it a boot."

"You can't put her in the trunk." By this time the girl has walked up to the car and is checking us out. And I am checking her out. Though I try not to stare. I don't want to freak her out. It's hard enough for a guy to hitchhike, it's probably a nightmare for a college girl.

Richard jumps out of the car then and says hello. "Name's Richard and that's Buddy." I am relieved. I figure if he's introducing me, he isn't going to kick me out. "Where you going?"

"New York City," she says. "But wherever is fine." I think that is a strange answer, but a good one. "I'm Claire." She has one hand on her hip, head cocked. "Damn, what a sweet ride," she says, staring at the TR-4 like it is a painting in a museum.

"It's gonna be cramped," Richard says, "but we can do it." He motions to Claire to come around the back of the Triumph. Cars are whizzing by and a light cold rain has begun to fall. "Put your suitcase in the trunk, and Buddy, put your backpack in there too." Now we are all standing in the cold. Claire, I notice, is almost as tall as me and I'm right at six feet. We're definitely going to be cramped. "We have to decide who gets to sit behind the seat." The space behind the seat is long and very narrow, like a coffin.

"I'll do it," I pipe up, surprising myself. "But I get to keep the blanket."

"Sounds good to me," Claire says. "I can also drive if you want. My boyfriend has a Jag."

"I may take you up on that," Richard says. "We've still got a few hundred miles to go."

As I struggle to fit into the space behind the seats, I think about what Claire has just said. Shit, she has a boyfriend.

For some reason, the wind and cold are more intense in the cramped space behind the bucket seats. I try to close my eyes and maybe sleep, but even though I haven't slept for a day and a half, I'm not tired. Weary, yes, but not sleepy. I realize there's a difference. I can hear Claire and Richard chatting away in the front, but the blowing wind makes it impossible to hear exactly what they are talking about. They look, though, like they are getting into it, Richard gesturing with the hand that isn't on the steering wheel. Of course, I am jealous. I want to be having that conversation—with Claire, not Richard. That's how quickly my damn allegiance can change. Show me a good-looking girl, and I become an idiot.

After an hour or so, I can't take it anymore and tap Richard on the shoulder. "I have to pee," I shout.

"Damn. Why didn't you do that when we were in the restaurant?"

"Forgot," I yell.

"Well, just fucking hold it."

Claire says something to him then, and Richard gradually slows down, looking for a place to pull over.

"What'd you say to him?" I ask Claire when I had unfolded myself out of the car.

"I just told him I had to go too." Then she laughs. And so do I.

We both make our way off to the side of the road where there are some scrub trees we can hide behind. Out of the corner of my eye I see Claire squatting. I turn away. When we get back to the car, Richard says he's tired again, the caffeine has worn off and one of us needs to drive. Claire's all over it. "I'll drive," she barks before I can open my mouth. Now I'll have to contort myself into the crawl space again.

"Okay," Richard says. "Don't speed, though. You get a ticket, you pay. I'm going to crash out in the back."

"Yes!" I say more loudly than I meant to.

"What's with you?" Richard asks.

"Nothing, man. Just a little punchy." I am not about to tell him, or Claire (especially Claire) that I can't wait to sit next to this girl, and maybe even come up with something halfway intelligent to say to her. I turn to Claire, as Richard climbs into the back. "Didya ever read that book? *On The Road*? Jack Kerouac? It's one of my favorites." As soon as I stop talking, I feel foolish.

"Mine too," Claire says.

After we've driven a few miles in silence, the rain turns to snow. Not real heavy, but enough so that it is hard to see very far ahead. Claire has her hands clamped to the wheel. She's a good driver, not hesitant at all, but has to slow it down now as the snow begins to collect on our hats and shoulders. "Damn," Claire mutters. "What kind of dumb motherfucker drives a car without a top in the middle of winter?"

I laugh out loud. "Yeah, pretty damn dumb," I say.

"I can hear you, you know," Richard shouts out from the back. "Fuckheads." We all start laughing then. "Now let me sleep," he says. "I'm going to get the top fixed soon."

"That helps a lot," Claire says. Richard lies back down.

We press on through the snow, the windshield wipers working hard to keep the falling snow cleared off. There's a little bit of heat coming from the vents near the floor, and I wiggle my feet right up close to the one on my side. At least I'm not freezing—not yet.

"You gotta talk to me," Claire says. "Keep me awake."

I struggle to come up with something, and then say, "So, what's your major?"

"No, you didn't really ask me that."

"Kind of stupid, huh?"

"Worst pick-up line of all time. Try again." She looks over at me. I see she's not angry, but also not all that pleased.

"Okay, so what kind of music do you like?"

"Better," she says. "Worth an answer anyway."

"So?"

"I like Miles Davis, Coltrane, Joan Baez. Sometimes Dylan."

"Only sometimes?"

"The man can't sing for shit."

"Sacrilege," I say. "*Bringing it All Back Home* got me through my sophomore year. Sat up all night listening to it."

"Enough small talk," Claire says then. "Tell me something that makes you sad."

"Really?" I'm not used to talking about my feelings.

"Really."

I hesitate, then say, "Well, I guess I'm scared of being a fuck-up. Disappointing my parents. That makes me sad."

"Bullshit," Claire says. "Forget about your parents.

They're not you. Tell me something that makes *you* sad, Buddy. Something deep down."

It's the middle of the night, I'm driving through a snowstorm with people I've just met and my head is in someplace it's never been before and, in this moment, for some reason, I feel released, and so I say, "It makes me sad when I think about how I'm the only person who's ever going to really understand what it feels like to be inside of my skin, inside of my brain, looking out."

"Yeah, I get that," Claire says. "We're all fucking alone in this life, aren't we?"

"Do you think there's any way to get out?" I ask her.

"Aside from dying?"

"Yeah, aside from that."

"I don't really know. Maybe if you find someone just like yourself."

"Has that ever happened to you?"

"Fuck no."

I laugh, amused by her rough language. I can't take my eyes off her. I could fall in love with this person in about twelve seconds. "Now it's my turn."

"For what?" She brushes a lock of hair away from her eyes. We're both pretty soaked by now. But I don't much care.

"For me to ask a deep question."

"Go for it," she says.

"First, I want to ask another dumb question."

"If you must."

"Where do you go to college?"

"What makes you think I go to college?"

"I just assumed you did."

"That is dumb."

"So you don't?"

"Didn't say that either."

"Come on, Claire, stop fucking with me."

She reaches over and touches my knee. "Look, you seem like a nice kid, but we need to get one thing straight between us."

I am very conscious of her hand on my knee. "What's that?"

"I am never going to fuck you. So get that out of your mind."

I feel myself blush, glad that Claire can't see. "Who said anything about that? I thought we were just talking. You know, killing time on the road."

"Whatever you say." She pulls her hand back off my knee. "And I don't go to college. Not my thing."

"So, what do you do?"

"Whatever I want."

"Do you have a job?"

"Sure. I wait tables. Is that okay with you?"

"Why are you getting angry with me?"

"Who says I'm angry?"

"I think I just did."

She laughs then. "So you did."

"Should I just shut up?"

"No, no. Forget it. I'm feeling a little raw is all. Sometimes I don't play well with others. At least that's what my teachers always wrote on my report cards."

"I thought we were getting along just fine."

"Maybe I'm a little touchy about the college thing."

"How come?" I was starting to breathe normally again.

"Cause everybody expected me to go. And I got accepted at a few good schools."

"Like where?"

"Doesn't matter where."

"Sorry."

"The thing was I had no damn idea of why I should go to college for four years. I didn't know what I wanted to do with my life. I didn't want to be anything in particular. I'm 24 now and I still don't."

"So what happened?"

"I just split."

"Split?"

"Yeah, the night before I was supposed to leave for school, I took off for the city. Didn't even tell my parents. Never looked back."

"Amazing," I say.

"You're a bit vocabulary challenged, aren't you?"

"I guess."

"I rest my case."

"So then what happened?"

"There is no then. There's never any then. Just now. Here. Driving on the fucking turnpike."

"My 'now' always ends up feeling stuck in cement."

"That's cause you're not making your own choices. You know what your boy Dylan says."

"He says lots of things."

"'You shouldn't let other people get your kicks for you' is what he says."

The snow is coming down even harder. I can barely see three feet in front of us. "You okay with the driving?" I ask Claire.

"Getting a bit hairy," she says, as she looks out over the steering wheel. "Road's getting slick."

"Maybe we should stop."

"And then what, sit here and let the snow bury our asses?"

"Better than crashing." Just then I feel the car slide sideways. I look over at Claire. She pulls the wheel to the left, gently, calmly, and the little car comes back into line.

"Keep your eyes out for a good place to stop," she says. "A restaurant or something."

"Probably all closed now."

"Just look, dammit. Mister Negativity."

"Fuck you," I say, surprising myself once again. "You don't know me."

"Okay, sorry," Claire says, and takes her eyes off the road for a second to look at me. "I'm being a dick."

"I know how that goes," I say, and try to brush the snow off the side window so I can see. "Let's just get off at the next exit, there's bound to be someplace we can stop."

"Gotcha," Claire says, peering out over the steering wheel. "What about sleepy-head?" She gestures with her thumb over her shoulder.

"Let's not bother him. One way or another we have to stop." It's then I see the sign, half covered in blowing snow: *Food and Lodging. Exit Ahead.* "Would you look at that shit."

"Very cool," Claire says, and guides the little car to the off-ramp. "Now we just have to hope there's someplace open."

"There will be," I say. "Don't worry."

"Look who's positive now." She's smiling.

"Over there!" I point toward a neon sign ahead.

As we drive closer, the letters arrange themselves into *Motel 6.* And beneath that a blinking vacancy sign. "I thought we were looking for a restaurant," Claire says. "What are we gonna do in a motel?"

"What does anybody do in a motel?" My weariness is catching up with me again.

"I told you about that."

"I meant sleep. You know, rest. Damn."

"Relax, Buddy. I'm just messing with you." Claire chuckles. "Looks like it's the Motel 6 for us." She pulls into the lot and up to a sign that tells us it's the office. There's a light on. Our luck is holding, though this was not how I planned on spending the night and my parents might now be worried, as I had called them before I left to say I'd be home on the 20th, which I am pretty sure is today. It's then that I feel a shift in weight behind us and Richard sits up and rubs his eyes. "What the fuck is this?" are his first words.

"Motel 6," I say.

"I can see that. But what the hell are we doing here?"

"We're gonna find out if they have any rooms." Claire says.

"Why?" Richard looks genuinely confused.

"The snow, man," I say and then chuckle nervously. "Not like a snowman with a carrot for a nose, and a hat and stuff. That's not what I was saying."

"What the fuck is he babbling about?" he asks Claire.

"The snow, Richard, the snow. The roads were too slick to drive. So here we are. Live with it."

Richard looks around at the snow drifting around us. "Okay then. We'll stay here for the night."

"Thanks for your permission," Claire says. "Big of you."

"So, who's going in?" I point to the office.

"I will," Claire says, and gets out of the car. Richard and I follow suit.

"No," Richard says, "I should probably go."

"Why's that?" Claire asks.

"You know," Richard gestures at the three of us. "It won't look right."

"How come?" I ask.

"He thinks a motel manager won't rent a room to a chick?" Now I can see that Claire is getting angry, jaw locked. "Right, Richard?"

"I just think it will look odd, your renting a room for the three of us."

"I wasn't planning on telling him there were three of us." She waits and lets that sink in. "I'll just say I'm a single college gal driving myself home to see good ole Ma and Pa. After I get the keys, you guys will sneak in. Save us a shitload of money."

"Sounds like you've done this before," I say.

"Maybe," Claire says. "Just lay low for a bit." Then she walks off toward the office and Richard and I get back in the car and slink down so we won't be noticed.

"She's something else," I say after a time.

"Yeah, but what?" Richard seems pissed off.

I spy Claire then walking out of the office, smile on her face. She holds up a large hotel key fob for us to see and ambles off toward a row of tiny cabins. Richard and I watch as she turns the lock and walks into the one with a number three on it. I wonder how we are all going to fit in that miniature cabin and where we will sleep. I'm excited to see what happens next.

First thing we do is crank up the heat as far as it will go. "Whew," Claire says, as the cabin warms, "feels good to have a roof over our heads."

"I know, I know. I should have had the top fixed," Richard says. "Stop busting my balls."

"Not what I meant," Claire says. "I'm just glad to be inside. God knows where we'd be if you hadn't picked us up."

"Yeah, well I guess we're even then." Richard peels off his jacket and throws it on the floor near the wall heater where it might dry by morning. I follow suit. And then we all just stand there looking around. There's one double bed, an oily brown-leather couch, a wood laminate dresser with a battered television on top, which I'm guessing will not pick up any stations, and off to the side is a closet and a mini-bathroom. I'm hoping there is hot water for a shower. There's a mist in the air from the blowing heat and our drying jackets. I can smell what I think is sour milk, but there is no refrigerator here. Maybe it's only the sad odor of hundreds of weary travelers.

It's the first time I've had a full look at Richard and Claire. It's hard to see when everyone is all bundled up.

Richard is stockier than I first thought, more muscular. He probably works out, I think; something I've been meaning to start. I glance now at Claire, don't want to stare, at least don't want her to catch me staring. She's even prettier than I first thought, though I imagine some people wouldn't think so. Her hair is dark and wiry and her eyebrows are bushy, like they almost meet in the middle. "Relax," I mumble. "Just fucking relax, man."

"What'd you say?" Claire asks.

"Nothing, just talking to myself." I walk over to the dresser and turn on the television. Like I thought, all I get is fuzz and static. I switch it off.

"So, what's the deal?" Richard asks, gesturing around the small space. "Who sleeps where?"

"Doesn't matter to me," I say.

"I'll take the couch," Richard says. "You two take the bed."

I swallow hard. "That's okay, I can sleep on the floor."

"What's the matter, you scared of bunking with me?" Claire says. "I won't bite. Probably."

"I'm not scared. But what about the blankets? I mean, what are we gonna do about the blankets?"

I hear Richard laugh. "You're a piece of work, man. Just go for it." He kicks off his shoes and lies down on the ugly couch, adjusts a throw pillow behind his head.

Claire opens the closet door and pulls out two khaki-colored blankets and tosses one over Richard on the couch, then pitches the other one on to the bed. "Everybody happy now?"

"Yeah," I say, once again at a loss for words. "Damn, I'm hungry," is all I come up with. "I could eat a horse."

"I'm going to take a shower," Claire announces, and my brain turns to the same out-of-focus fuzz I saw on the old tv set. She kicks off her shoes, and heads into the bathroom.

Richard is already snoring away on the couch. I don't know what to do with myself. I can hear the shower running and can't help picturing Claire in there with the hot water running down her back. There's not even any place to sit, so I park myself on the edge of the bed. I don't want to fully lie down, cause that would feel weird when Claire gets out of the shower. And then what am I supposed to do? And what the hell will she be wearing when she gets out—if she will be wearing anything at all, and I know that I am spinning out of control so take a few deep breaths and tell myself to relax, to grow the hell up. This is an adventure. Isn't that why I started hitchhiking in the first place? I could have taken the damn Greyhound if I wanted to be bored. This, all this, is definitely not boring.

Fifteen minutes later Claire emerges from the shower, a white towel wrapped completely around her torso, another one wound around her hair. "Damn, that felt good," she says. She sits on the edge of the bed, turned away from me. "You should try it. There's hot water left."

"Maybe in the morning."

"Suit yourself." Then, in a couple quick moves, she pulls the towels away and slips under the covers. "I'm going down."

"Good night," I say, wishing I had something more clever to add, but before I can think of anything, Claire is snuggled down and turned away. I don't even get a good-night.

Once I'm sure Claire is asleep (she's breathing deeply—not quite a snore), I strip off my damp jeans and sweatshirt and lay them out on the floor. I've got another shirt in my backpack, but the jeans I'll have to wear again. In only my boxers, I go wash up in the bathroom. I stare at myself in the mirror and feel disoriented. My hair looks greasy, plastered down, and my skin is breaking out again. Why would someone like Claire ever be interested in someone as unattractive as I am? "Fuck it," I say, and scrub my face hard with the little soap the motel has left for us. I don't have a toothbrush, though I see that there is one sitting inside a glass on the sink. I realize it must be Claire's and am tempted to use it, but I resist and just swirl some water from the tap around in my mouth. I don't drink too much because I don't want to have to get up in the middle of the night to pee.

I tiptoe out and crawl into my side of the bed and pull the rough blanket up over my bare skin. Claire has claimed the top sheet. I lie on my back, pretty sure I will not be able to sleep. Besides the fact that I am sleeping in the same bed with a woman (something I have never done), I also have all sorts of random and mostly troubling thoughts running through my brain. But before I realize it I'm opening my eyes to a new, and sunny, day.

"Richard split," is the first thing Claire says to me.

I sit up with my back against the headboard. "What do you mean?"

"He's gone, out of here." She points outside. "No car, no ride. We're fucked."

I rub my eyes and try to absorb the situation. I stare at Claire who is wearing tight jeans and a clean white tee shirt. Her hair is pulled back into a long ponytail. "Why would he do that?" is all I can think to say.

"Who knows? Maybe he was tired of hauling us around." She walks over and sits down beside me on the bed. "It's not like he owed us anything."

Claire is so close I can feel the heat of her on my bare skin, she smells of soap and, for some reason, oranges. I feel myself getting hard under the blanket. "So, what do we do now?"

Claire turns and looks directly at me. "Who says there's a 'we'? You and I just met, honey." She puts her hand on my shoulder. It feels warm and electric at once. "We each have to decide what we want."

"I know what I want." My voice is husky.

"Oh yeah?" Claire looks down at my lap and chuckles. "I can see that." She brushes her hand down my arm.

"Sorry about that," I say.

"No need to be sorry. It's natural. You're a guy."

"Yeah. Guess I am." I want to run and hide. "Could you reach me my pants?"

"Is that what you really want?" Claire asks, smiling. "Or is there something else? You can say it."

"I don't know. What?"

"If you don't ask for what you want in this life, you don't ever get it."

I look up at her face, then lower my eyes to her small breasts pressing against her tee shirt, gather my courage, and say, "I want you to touch me."

"That's the way." She pulls the blanket back. "I'll take care of you. But stay still."

Her warm hand finds me. I want to shout and cry at the same time. But I keep quiet, sensing that is what Claire wants from me. She strokes me gently, like nothing I have ever felt before. I'm not a virgin, but my experience with girls has always been back-seat rushed and awkward. This is different, this is perfect. I want it to last forever at the same time I want to explode.

"Is this okay?" Claire says.

"God, yes." I look directly in her eyes then. They are deep brown, almost black. She's no longer smiling. I reach out to touch her.

"No," Claire says. "Just you." And she leans over and kisses me dryly on the lips.

I can hold it no longer. My world has contracted to this one ecstatic moment and I can't stop myself from screaming out as my body shudders with pleasure.

"What the hell's going on?" I hear then, as if from a distance. I slide down under the cover as Claire pulls her hand away.

"Oh, hi there, Richard," Claire says. "We thought you had abandoned us."

"Why would I do that? Just went out to get us some breakfast." He holds up two brown paper bags. "Coffee and donuts. That is, if you two are interested in such things." He laughs. "What's with him?" Richard glances over to where I'm huddled in the bed.

"Touch of fever," Claire says. "Too much activity."

"I'll bet," Richard says.

I slide to the other side of the bed, then slip out, back turned and skitter off to the bathroom. I think I hear them both laughing behind me, but I don't care. When I look at myself in the mirror, I can hardly believe it's me. Something big has happened. "I'm going to take a shower," I call out. Nobody answers.

When I get out, I quickly pull on my jeans and a blue tee shirt that I like. Richard and Claire are sitting on the couch sipping their coffees. "Yours is over there." Richard points toward the bureau. I grab the cardboard coffee cup and the jelly donut that's sitting next to it. "Thanks, man. I'm glad you didn't leave us."

Richard nods, smirks. "The snow's almost all gone. We should be able to make Philly in three hours."

"Cool," I say, but what I'm thinking is that I don't want this trip to end. Not now, not when everything is finally opening up, not ever.

"So, eat up and let's get on the move," Richard says. He turns to Claire then. "How much do we owe you for the room?"

"You don't owe me anything," she says to Richard. "You're paying for the ride." She looks at me, as I wipe sugar from my mouth. "Buddy, you can give me ten bucks if you've got it."

"I have it," I say, and reach for my wallet, then hand her a ten-dollar bill. I don't tell her that it is the last of my money.

"When I hand the bill to her, she leans over and whispers in my ear, "Don't ever forget me."

"Come on people, let's go," Richard says. "Time's a wasting."

◊ ◊ ◊

It's Claire's turn to ride in the back. I volunteer to do it, but she waves me off. "I can manage." She slides her long body in headfirst. "I've been in worse places."

Richard drives and I ride shotgun. The sun warms us as we get back on the Pennsylvania Turnpike and Richard guns the engine. I should be happy, I should have the biggest grin on my face that I've ever had. But instead I feel sort of lonely and sad. Maybe that's my default setting. I'd like to talk to Claire about it, but when I look over my shoulder, she's huddled up with her eyes closed, and I don't want to bother her. I think about talking to Richard, but he's focused on the road ahead, like he's part of the snappy TR-4, both of them out for a morning run. I've got to stay inside my own head—a place I'm still not comfortable. I sit there worrying about going home and having to explain myself once again to my parents, which will probably end up with shouts and accusations. "Not this time," I say, apparently out loud.

"What?" Richard yells above the sound of the wind blowing over the windshield.

"Nothing," I shout back. "No big deal."

Richard turns back to the road, pulling up and around a blocky sedan. I lean back and stare out the window at the passing scenery, which is not much to look at in this part of the state. I think then about what happened this morning; it was a big deal for me. I'm not even sure why. It's not about words or promises or even sex. I don't even want to name it, and I know that I will probably never tell another soul in the world about what happened—at least not till I'm much older and looking back at my life. "Hey Richard," I yell out again. "You know what?" I don't wait for a response. "I think I'm going to move to California."

Richard turns and smiles, "Whatever you say, man."

Paternity

At First

I wasn't sure I wanted to be a father. Didn't feel strongly about it one way or the other. But Annie was pregnant, so there was that. She didn't get that way by herself. We decided to go ahead with it. There wasn't an actual discussion or anything. Annie and I never had those. But we did sign up for a Lamaze class, which I grudgingly went to with her. We practiced correct breathing, and I learned how to be a "supportive partner."

After a longer-than-normal pregnancy, the day finally arrived. We were both scared shitless as we drove through rush-hour Philadelphia traffic to University Hospital. Annie was clenching her teeth, then screaming when the contractions came. I patted her knee; she glared at me like she wanted to murder me. I didn't take it too seriously. Lamaze had warned me about this. "Just do everything you can to make her feel safe," they told us husbands.

Like the pregnancy, the delivery was long and painful, lasting more than 14 hours. Annie called me a motherfucker and a cunt, both of which I thought were inaccurate, but I didn't say anything. She also swatted my hand away when I tried to put ice-chips in her mouth. "You smell like smoke, asshole," she yelled. I told the attending nurse I needed to go out for a cigarette break. She too glared at me.

But I was there when the baby slithered out. Annie even let me hold her hand. And when they handed this squalling little baby girl to her, we both cried. Up till this moment, it had all been about me, now I knew everything would change. It was like shedding my old skin, an opening and a closing all in one moment.

We named her Josephine, which was the one thing we had decided on ahead of time. It was gonna be Joseph if it was a boy, named after my grandfather. But like everything previous, even getting the baby out of the hospital didn't go smoothly. She had a slight yellow cast to her skin, which the Doc said was jaundice and that she'd have to remain in the hospital, in one of those incubation pods for a time. This didn't appear to bother Annie; she smiled lazily, still under the influence of the epidural, as the nurse plucked the baby from her arms. But I was worried, even angry, though I wasn't sure why. I felt like it was on me to protect this precious newborn, and so started yelling at our obstetrician. "Tell me the truth, man. I'm not going anywhere till you tell me everything is going to be okay."

"Can't do that," he said.

"Fuck you can't."

"Go be with your wife, Bud. She needs you more than the baby does right now."

"I doubt it," I said.

He shrugged. "I thought you were one of the good guys."

"Well, now you know," I said and turned away. *What the fuck am I doing?* I remember thinking. *Don't be a jerk.* But instead I walked out of the hospital onto the early morning city streets and wandered around the West Philadelphia neighborhood. People were going to work or to school or arriving at the hospital with their own problems; buses, delivery trucks, and cars hurried by. The air was gray and heavy with exhaust fumes, but still I breathed it in and felt better. I decided I needed to call my father. Which was sort of strange in that I hardly had spoken to him in the last few years. We had our differences, not the least of which was that he and my mother had made it very clear they didn't approve of my youthful marriage or my choice of mates. They were probably right, but it had caused a serious rift in our already shaky relationship. Still, I looked for a phone booth.

Dad didn't seem surprised to get my call. "What do you need?" was the first thing he asked.

I told him about what was going on and even about how angry I was. "What should I do, Dad? I'm going crazy here."

There was a brief pause. I imagined my father sitting in

his medical office, puffing on the ever-present pipe, could almost smell the tang of tobacco. "Just relax, Buddy. Take a deep breath. They know what they're doing at that hospital. You'll be taking that baby and your wife home in no time."

"Her name's Josephine."

"Good name, son."

"Thanks, Dad. I'll talk to you later."

"Anytime," he said. And in that moment I knew something else about being a father: it never ends.

I was a lousy husband, but a pretty good father. At least I thought I was. What I didn't realize at the time was that you can't be one without the other. By the time I figured that out, it was too late. Still, I told myself right from the start that I was going to be a better parent than mine had been to me. Maybe every new parent thinks that. For me, it meant that I was going to be fully invested in my daughter's upbringing. I'd be there for her—all the time. And we'd talk when she was old enough—about everything and anything she wanted to talk about. And I'd encourage her creativity by reading books to her and playing music and dancing around with her. I did those things and I felt like I was becoming a better version of myself. I was happy; and I believe my daughter was too. Not so sure about my wife. She seemed a bit down, gloomy and distant. I should have talked to her about how she was feeling, but I didn't.

We were living at the Jersey Shore in those early years after Joey was born. I had given up my teaching job at a public high school, because the Philadelphia neighborhood where we lived didn't feel safe to my wife. Annie was originally from a small town in upstate New York and was nervous around all the dark-skinned people who were our neighbors. She said that she thought they were all staring at her. "This isn't a good place to raise a baby. Not if you have a choice," she told me, with that hard set to her jaw I'd come to recognize. To be honest, I hadn't married Annie for any of the right reasons. I was attracted to her because she was pretty and because I didn't know what to do with my life. Annie was nice to me (at first), and I thought that was enough. I never knew why she married me.

At the beach, I was content and went for long walks with Joey secured in a carrier on my back. She was a good rider, never fussed, except when she got hungry and then we would stop at the local drugstore/food shop and buy treats. I liked how the older lady cashier at the store would smile at me and fuss over Josephine, who now had flocks of curly blonde hair and was, in my opinion, a beautiful child. The cashier lady seemed to think the same. Being a father, I thought, was the best thing that ever happened to me.

But being a parent also means that you have to make a

living. There were limited opportunities for work on Long Beach Island in the off-season. The place only thrived between the end of the school year and Labor Day. After a couple dead-end gigs as a truck driver and a dishwasher, I decided I'd have to figure out some way to work for myself and not be tied down to regular hours. Otherwise, I couldn't spend quality time with my kid. A new friend, who had lived on the coast his whole life, took me out clamming in his boat. He pointed to some of the other boats around us. "They go full-time at it," he told me.

"At what?"

"Clamming."

"Really? You mean you can make a living digging clams?"

"Not just digging. You gotta rake in the winter and tread in the summer. Some of the old-timers still use tongs."

I didn't know quite what he was talking about but decided right then and there that I wanted to be a full-time clammer. "Wanta sell me your boat?" I asked.

He didn't, but helped me find one, the kind that all the commercial clammers used. It was made from cedar, with a flat bottom so it could maneuver in shallow waters, and was painted green, with an old Johnson outboard for power. I loved that boat. It took me a while to get the hang of clamming. It was hard work. You couldn't make a living at it unless you were bringing in more than a thousand clams a day. My first day, I got twelve. Ten the next day. Forty after that. And after a couple months, when my muscles were stronger, and I figured out where to go and when the tides were right, I was doing it for real. Selling my burlap bags full of clams every day at the dock and satisfied as I'd ever been with any job.

But after three years on the coast my wife was unhappy. She told me she wanted to leave, felt constrained on this barren and winter-cold island. "I've got no friends here," she whined. I did feel sorry for her—in an abstracted sort of way. "Let's move, Buddy. Please."

"I don't want to move," I said. "I like it here. Pretty soon we'll have enough money to maybe buy a house."

"And then what?"

"Then we'll be set. You know, maybe have another kid."

"I don't want that. Not here. This is a dead-end for me."

"What would you do someplace else?" I asked. "You've never really had a job or anything."

"I've been raising a baby. In case you hadn't noticed." She turned away from me. "Screw you, Buddy. I've had it."

"What's that supposed to mean?"

"It means I'm leaving. With or without you. And I'm taking Joey."

"You wouldn't do that," I said.

"Watch me." She looked me dead in the eye.

"This is our life here. What about my boat? What about walking on the beach?"

"That's all you care about, isn't it?"

"What is?"

Annie stepped right up to me, inches from my face. "It's all about what *you* want. You don't give a shit about me—or your daughter."

"That's not true. Who do you think I'm doing all this for?" I waved my arm around the room. Joey was playing with blocks in the corner. A Joni Mitchell record was playing softly. Annie said nothing; held her gaze on me. She was a hard woman.

I knew I was lost. It was Annie and my kid or a place and work I loved. Tomorrow I would put the boat up for sale. "Would you want another kid if we leave?" I said.

"We'll see," she said, and walked back into the bedroom.

We moved across the country to Seattle. My best buddy, Pete Curry, who I'd met in grad school, lived there now. He told me a lot of young, progressive people were moving to Seattle, and that you could even buy a house pretty cheaply. "What about work?" I asked him.

"You can work with me," he said. "I've got a little construction company going. Buying up old houses and rehabbing them."

"Glad we got those fine art degrees."

"Yeah, right." We both laughed.

Once we were ensconced in Seattle I thought Annie was now satisfied. Or at least she should have been. But she was still moping around. "Now what is it? What's wrong?" I asked in one of our late-night sullen arguments. The kind where we didn't say much, until one of us broke down and said something poisonous.

"Nothing," she said, staring into a book I suspected she wasn't really reading. Josephine was asleep in a back bedroom. I had read to her for an hour before she went down. I did it every night. Now we were reading *The Little Prince*.

"Seems like something."

"I said it's nothing."

"Guess you don't like it here either."

"Seattle's fine."

"Then what, damnit?"

"You really want to know?" I didn't answer but didn't look away. "It's us, Buddy."

"Us?"

"Yeah. You and me. It isn't working." Her tone dropped a note. "You know that's true, don't you? We make each other feel shitty."

As soon as those words were spoken I knew she was right. Once things go dark like that, there's nothing much left to say. We'd been torturing each other for way too long.

We barely spoke most days, except to figure out who was watching our daughter. "What about Joey?" I asked.

"She'll stay with me," Annie said. "I'm her mother."

"And I'm her damn father. You're not taking her away from me. No way."

"I don't want to fight about this, Buddy. A young girl belongs with her mom." She stopped and looked up at me. I was standing now, hands on hips. "You'll still get to spend time with her. I wouldn't take her away from you."

"Damn right you won't." I took a breath, tried to rein myself in. I had to stay calm, not fly off in a rage like I usually did with her. "Look, Ann, how about this? We each have her every other week."

"I don't like you calling Josephine 'her.'"

"What the fuck are you talking about?"

"You said we'd share 'her,' like she's some damn stranger. An impersonal pronoun."

Again I took a breath. "Right, got it." Another breath. "So, can we agree to that arrangement? Every other week *Josephine* will stay with one of us. Let's not make this harder than it already is. Can we do that please? Please."

"Maybe," Annie said. "I'll think about it." Then she went off to the bedroom and I was left with my thoughts and fears. I knew one thing, though: whatever I had to do, nobody was going to take my daughter away from me.

We spent two more awkward weeks together, where we mostly tried to avoid each other. Strangely, Ann and I kept sleeping together, and even more strange, the sex was better than it had ever been. I knew I would miss that part.

Eventually, I found a new apartment for myself and Joey. It wasn't much, a basement with one tiny bathroom, a serviceable kitchen, and a bedroom for Josephine. I'd sleep on the ugly yellow corduroy couch in the front room. I liked the place, liked that it was mine alone. And for a time the arrangement with Annie seemed to be working. We'd have a handoff every Sunday night, during which time we were cordial to one another, but didn't ask too many questions, though I had a lot of them going through my head.

Months passed. Luckily for me, the nice older woman who I was renting the basement apartment from and who lived on the top floors, was also more than willing to be a baby-sitter for Josephine while I was off at work. The house-flipping gig with Pete was working out well, and I figured once Joey was in kindergarten, I would have enough money saved to rent a bigger place, or maybe even put a down payment on a house. A working person could buy a house in Seattle pretty cheaply at that time. I felt like I was turning a corner, maybe even moving toward being a responsible adult. My parents would have been proud.

Annie called and said she wanted to talk, if that was okay with me. "Maybe when I drop Joey off next week?"

"No problem," I said. "Anything special?"

"Nothing special. Just need to let you know about some things that are going on."

"That sounds ominous."

"No big deal," she said quietly. "Just want to keep you in the loop."

"Okay, cool. So, I'll see you Sunday."

"See you Sunday," she said and hung up.

"Fuck me," I said out loud. "What now?"

Josephine jumped up into my arms as soon as I opened the door. She was starting to sprout, long and lanky already. I had to admit she looked a lot like her mom. "Hi Daddy," she squealed. "Are we having ice cream? Can we go to the doggie park?"

I laughed and set her down. "First, we'll make dinner."

"I want hot dogs and soda. Okay, Daddy?" She didn't wait for an answer and ran past me to her bedroom.

I turned then to Annie, who was still waiting in the doorway. "Don't worry, I'm not going to feed her junk."

"I know," she said. "You're a good father."

"Really? Where'd that come from?"

"It's something I've been thinking about lately. Josephine's lucky to have you, that's all. Not every father loves his daughter, you know. Mine didn't. Asshole didn't even stick around past my fifth birthday. Called me once when I turned thirteen, told me he'd moved to Mexico and that maybe I could come visit him there. That was the last we heard from him."

"Do you want to come in? You said we needed to talk."

"Did I?" She moved inside and looked around. "Your place is looking good."

"Yeah, I like it. And Mrs. McCarthy has been a big help, watching Joey when I'm at work."

"Must be nice," Annie said in a dreamy sort of voice.

"Is something wrong?" I asked.

"Not really."

"Not really?"

"Can I sit down, Buddy? I'm feeling a little lightheaded."

"Sure. Sit. I'll get you a glass of water."

She plopped down on the couch before I could move the blankets I had piled up on it. She didn't seem to notice, just fell back onto them. "I don't need water, honey."

"Honey?"

"Yeah, you're still my honey, aren't you?"

"What's going on, Ann? You're starting to worry me."

"Just starting?" She grinned.

"Talk to me," I said. I could hear Joey in the back bedroom, chattering happily to her Raggedy Ann doll.

"Well, it's about you and me," she said. "I've been thinking a lot about us."

"About us?"

"Please, Buddy, stop repeating everything I say. Just listen, will you?"

"Sorry." I pulled up a spindly kitchen chair and sat down opposite her. "I'm listening."

"So, I think we should get back together."

"Get back together?"

"You're doing it again," she muttered.

My mind was racing. "What the hell, Annie? Where did this come from?" She slumped further down into the couch and blankets. I stood up and grabbed hold of the crumpled covers and pulled them out from under her. She didn't seem to notice. "You were the one who decided we made each other miserable. Do you want to go back to that?"

"Well, maybe we've changed. You know, grown up a little."

"I doubt that," I said, realizing in the moment that I was reverting to mean Buddy, the Buddy I was with her, and I didn't like it. I sat back down and crossed one leg over the other and waited.

"There's more to it than that," she finally said.

"Like what?"

"Well, like I'm pregnant."

I felt like someone punched me in the face. "That's insane," I said.

"Yeah, I know."

"You're sure?"

"Of course I'm sure. I'm not a fucking idiot."

"Shit. How far along are you?"

"I dunno. Probably like four or five months."

I stared at her. "I can't tell from looking at you."

"Well, you could if I took my clothes off." She laughed. "Don't worry, I'm not going to."

"Yeah, good. Don't think I'm ready for that."

"Damn, Buddy, I thought you were the one who wanted more kids."

"Not like this. Not now." I stopped and tried to gather my thoughts. "Anyway, are you sure it's mine? You know we haven't made love in a long time."

"Made love? I'm not sure we ever did that, sweetie."

"Okay. Well, I'll be more prosaic then."

"What's that mean?"

"It means, who else have you been fucking, Annie?"

"None of your damn business."

"Thought as much." I wanted her to leave. I wanted this all not to be happening.

"You can be a part of it or not. I don't really give a shit."

"Sweet," I said. "You always did have a way with words."

"Screw you, Buddy." She stood up and moved to the door, opened it, then turned back. "You better think hard about all this."

I didn't know what to say, so stood mute and stared at her.

"And don't feed my daughter hot dogs." She slammed the door on her way out.

Next

The second birth went much easier than the first. Annie called me at work. "It's time," is all she said. She didn't sound particularly concerned.

"I'm on my way," I told her, hung up, told Pete I had to split and jumped in my pickup and headed over to the basement apartment that Joey and I now shared with Ann. She was waiting outside when I got there.

"Mrs. McCarthy is watching Joey," she said and got into the truck. I didn't need to help her up.

We barely made it to the birthing clinic where we had arranged to have the delivery. No hospitals this time. Dr. Gold was waiting for us when we arrived. "You ready?" He greeted us with a wide smile and led Annie into the delivery room. Rosie was born twenty minutes later, dark-haired and squalling; no muss, no fuss. We named her after the nurse who assisted with the delivery, as we hadn't made any other plan. Dr. Gold, an older Jewish guy with a pencil mustache, asked me if I wanted to cut the umbilical cord and held up a pair of surgical scissors. I took a step toward him and my splayed-out wife but couldn't take another. I felt weak and dizzy. Rosie the nurse came over and took my arm. "Better go sit down, honey," she said.

"I'm okay," I said. But I knew I was not. Still, I was glad that the birth had gone well, and that Rosie looked healthy, which Dr. Gold assured us she was. And even Annie seemed pleased. I knew we had lots of shit to work out and was not at all confident that it would be possible. Still, we thanked the doc and Rosie, and were out of there in less than two hours. We even stopped at a fast-food restaurant on the way home, because Ann said she was hungry. We had Big Macs and fries and Annie ordered a small carton of milk, which for some reason I found jarring. This new life of ours was gonna be a trial. We both finished all of our meal, while I held the new baby in the crook of my arm.

As we drove back into the city, my mind drifted to one of the conversations I'd had with Annie well before this birth-day of "our" second daughter. It had occurred a couple weeks after she first announced that she was pregnant. She told me she was sorry she'd been "such a bitch" during our last conversation. I said I understood and that she was probably feeling a lot of pressure. This time I could definitely see that she was carrying, her tummy bulged against her tee-shirt.

We were once again sitting in my living room/bedroom. "You're looking healthy," I said.

"Yeah, I'm trying to be careful, you know."

"Where'd you get that shirt?" I asked. "I don't think I've seen it before." The tee-shirt was bright red and had the name of some band and a drawing of what looked like a jungle cat on it.

"Oh, this?" She pulled the edge of the shirt down and looked at it like she couldn't quite figure out where it had come from.

I waited.

"I think I bought it at this concert I went to. I just liked the color."

"So, you're going to rock concerts now."

"It's no big deal, Buddy."

"Didn't say it was." I couldn't stop staring at the brightly colored shirt and the belly it covered, the belly that carried a baby, possibly my baby. I was having trouble breathing. "Who'd you go with?"

"What do you mean?" She placed a hand on her stomach and turned away.

"Simple question," I said. "Who'd you go to the damn concert with?"

"Why are you getting mad?"

"I'm not."

"Doesn't sound like it."

"I'd appreciate an answer." I felt the heat rising in my chest.

"I didn't *go* with anybody."

"You went to a concert all by yourself?"

"Sort of." She plopped down on my couch. "Why are you interrogating me? I came here to talk. Thought we could have a civil conversation. Maybe talk about our future."

"What does 'sort of' mean?"

"Fine, then. If you must know, I met one of the guys in the band—Bing. He's the bass player. He invited me to their show. It was no big deal. Joey was with you and I just wanted to get out of the house. Happy now?"

"What'd you do after the show?"

"Please, Buddy. Stop."

I stared at her and waited, already knowing the answer to my question.

"I went backstage. Said hello. Hung out. Bing's a nice guy. You'd probably like him."

"Did you go home with him? This nice guy?"

"What if I did?" Hard Annie was re-emerging. "We're separated, remember?"

"Did you sleep with him?"

"This conversation is over." She stood and grabbed her jacket, a dark blue pea-coat that I had bought for her.

"Is he the only one?" I hissed at her, my anger barely contained.

She smiled. “Jealous, baby?”

“Fuck you.”

“You know what?” she said, as she opened the front door and turned back. “I’m having fun now. I never did when we were together. I wonder how you explain that.” She left before I could come up with an answer.

Now I was bringing that same woman and the new baby and all our massive emotional baggage back to my tiny basement apartment. Annie had not paid the rent on our old apartment for the last few months, so we couldn’t go there. “I wasn’t able to look for a job,” she’d explained. “I was like too upset after you left.”

I was terrified of what the next weeks and months would bring. I was especially worried about how Josephine would deal with this new living arrangement. She was almost five now and becoming smarter and more curious every day. I’d tried to prepare her for the new arrival but wasn’t at all sure she understood what it meant to have a baby sister. I tried to talk about it with Annie as we drove, make a plan. But all she said when I brought it up was, “Don’t worry. They’ll get along fine.” I was going to push it, but when I glanced over at her, holding Rosie, I felt a rare moment of compassion. I think that’s what it was. Maybe I just didn’t want to get into it with her anymore. We were both worn out.

When we arrived back at the apartment, Josephine was waiting with Mrs. McCarthy. They both rushed up to look at the baby resting in Annie's arms. "Can I hold her? Please?" Joey pleaded.

"Maybe later, honey," I said. "Rosie's sleeping now."

Annie knelt down. "She can do it. Joey should get to hold her baby sister." She handed the baby to her.

"I don't think this is a good idea," I said.

Mrs. M. looked nervous. "I'd better go back upstairs," she said.

Josephine clutched Rosie in her arms and stared at her with a mixture of what looked like wonder and anger. She started to carry the baby back into her bedroom. "Wait," I called, but Annie put a hand on my arm. "Let them go. They'll be fine."

Soon we heard the baby cry, and Joey carried her back, a sheepish look on her face. "I didn't do anything," she said.

Annie took Rosie and sat with her on the couch, pulling down a corner of her blouse to feed her. "Something's wrong," she said, as she brought Rosie to her breast. "Oh," Annie said, then, "Oh, that's funny, isn't it?" and put a finger in the baby's mouth. "Look at this." She held up a copper penny. "I wonder how this got in there?" Joey scurried back into her room.

We spent more than a year in that cramped apartment.

Conditions were so hectic that I sometimes forgot about how weird the whole situation was. Rosie's crib was pushed into a corner of Josephine's bedroom, while Annie and I shared the new hide-a-bed I bought. Her clothes were scattered all over the place. I was still working every day and also doing most of the cooking and food shopping, which I didn't mind. Enjoyed it really, and would take Josephine and Rosie, in her baby carriage, with me to the market. Annie said she was too tired to do any of that, even after months at home. I let it go. Mostly what I remember about that time was the fog-like silence between the two of us. It became a habit, self-protective. I had nothing I trusted myself to say to her, and apparently Annie felt the same. My life became the girls. I felt great joy when I was with them. And Joey had backed away from her early tortures of her baby sister once she saw that I wasn't about to abandon her. I rarely even thought about whether I was Rosie's biological father or not. I would be there for her the rest of my life.

When I told that to my mother in one of our weekly phone calls, she asked me, "So, she still won't tell you?" Mom refused now to call my wife by her name.

"I don't ask," I said. "It doesn't matter anymore."

"If you say so."

"I do."

"You don't want to get the paternity test?"

"Mom, please. Drop it."

"So, what will you tell Rosie when she grows up?"

"I'm going to hang up now."

"Tell Josephine I love her."

"And Rosie?"

"Sure, her too."

"Bye Mom." I replaced the receiver and shook my head. I should never have told my mother about the whole situation with Annie and our getting back together, but I couldn't help myself. When I was in the midst of turmoil and trying to decide the right thing to do, I almost automatically called my mother for advice and consolation. More the latter than the former. It was a long-standing habit, back to childhood. When I was sick or upset I went to Mom. And she comforted me, made me tea and toast. That's the way it was. She just wasn't doing quite as good a job now as she did when I had stomachaches.

When Rosie had her first birthday and with Joey approaching her sixth, Mrs. McCarthy's basement was no longer feasible. I don't know how we made it there as long as we did. But I found a house to buy in the same Wallingford neighborhood. It was a shabby foursquare, but the price was right and the girls would have their own bedrooms, and Annie and I could get the space we needed more than ever. I should have been more pleased than I was. I'd always wanted to be a homeowner but now that I was, I felt only a deepening of that hollow place in my gut. I needed to talk to someone about it, but instead choked the feelings down, and plowed ahead. Just like I'd been doing for the last couple years—and to be honest for most of the years before that. Something had to give. I decided to confide in the one person I knew who might understand, the one person I trusted not to lie to me.

I'd been friends with my business partner Pete Curry ever since grad school back in Cambridge. We'd met after one of the first lectures I attended when I'd stood up to challenge a comment the distinguished professor made. Pete waited for me outside and grabbed my arm. "Damn, man, that was exceptionally cool," he said.

I stepped back and checked him out. A tall guy, with long hair and a toothy smile. He had a red bandana tied around his wrist. I liked him right from the start. "What do you mean? What was cool?"

"How you spoke up. I mean that cat is famous. Nobody questions him."

"Well, I thought he was a bit off-base about the whole public-school thing is all. Not sure he's ever been in one."

"Let's get coffee, man. What's your name anyway?"

"Buddy," I told him and held out my hand.

"Pete," he said and, ignoring my outstretched hand, moved in for a hug.

We were pretty much inseparable after that. Hung out every day, shared stories about our families and about our inchoate plans and dreams. Pete told me he was gay, and that he hoped I was okay with that. I told him I was, and that I didn't really know any gay men. "Not many straight people do," Pete said, "Or at least they don't know they do."

On occasion I'd go with Pete to some of the Boston gay bars. It was weird for me, but I did love the dancing and didn't feel too out of place. Sometimes Pete would meet somebody and then I'd have to take the "T" back into Cambridge. It was on one of those nights when I stopped off at "Legal Seafoods" to get some clams and chips, that I met Annie. She was waitressing there while she took classes at B.U. I flirted with her, and she flirted back and wrote her phone number on the back of my tab. I thought she was pretty and kinda funny and so I called her the next day and before long we hooked up, then quickly and carelessly got married and pregnant, or the other way around. After I got my degree, we left Cambridge so I could take the teaching job in Philly and have money for the birth and all that real-world shit. Forgot about the dreams and even about my buddy Pete. Sometimes that's how it goes when you're not paying attention to where your life is headed.

But now Pete was back. We were business partners, learning the job as we went, making decent money and doing good work. He knew some of what had been going on with Annie and me, though I hadn't told him about the whole paternity business or about Bing the bass player, who I was pretty sure Ann was still seeing. Pete had so far stayed out of the whole mess. I could understand why. But now I needed him to step back up. I needed his help.

I asked Pete to meet me on a Saturday at Gasworks Park. Joey loved it there, perched right on the banks of Lake Union; she liked playing on all the weird industrial structures (now painted in bright pastel colors) left over from when the place was a functioning gas and coal plant. Rosie was still too young to do much of anything except watch her sister play and smile. Rosie was such an easy kid, never whined, rarely cried. I could take her anywhere. I let her scrabble around in a big sandbox when Pete showed up. We sat on a nearby bench, and I tried as best I could to tell him what was going on with me. He told me none of it was much of a surprise. "You've been moping around for months. I figured you'd tell me what was up when you were ready." He sat back and lit a cigarette, offered me the pack.

"Trying to quit, man," I said, but reconsidered and took one of the proffered Marlboro Reds. "What the fuck."

He held his lighter out for me. "So, talk to me. What's going on, brother?"

"Lots of stuff."

"Could you be a little more vague?"

"It's Annie," I said. "The whole family thing just isn't working with her."

"No surprise there. That woman reeks of trouble. Always has." He shuffled around on the bench to face me.

"I knew you were fucked the first time I met her back in Cambridge."

"Thanks for letting me know."

"I tried, man. You weren't hearing anything back then."

"Yeah, I know. I guess I didn't want anybody to tell me how blind I was."

"I get that. Been there myself. But why'd you let her back in? I thought you two had split for good."

"So did I. And I was fine with that. Felt better than I had in a long time."

"I know, man. You were solid. Happy as when I first saw your skinny ass back in school."

"Checking out my ass, were you?"

"You're not my type." We laughed then and I felt close to Pete, like we were still back there, and I was still full of hope.

"So why'd you let her back in?"

"She told me she was pregnant. What was I supposed to do?"

"Yeah, I can see how that would be hard."

"You know that Rosie might not be mine? She was also balling this bass player. Maybe others."

"I'm starting to hate that woman more than ever." Pete paused, seemed to be lost in thought, then said, "But it doesn't matter who's the sperm donor, does it?" We both stared at Rosie throwing handfuls of sand into the air.

"No. She's my daughter, Pete. Always will be."

"So, what's the problem?"

"The problem is her mother. I can't live like this anymore."

"Then don't."

"It's not that easy."

"Maybe it is." He ground out his smoke with the toe of his boot. "What does she want?"

"Who the fuck knows? We hardly speak to each other. She just mopes around the house all day, or else goes off for hours at a time without letting me know where she is. Which I don't really care about, except when she's supposed to be watching the kids."

"You mean she goes off and leaves them alone?"

I shook my head and looked down at my shoes. "I told her she had to stop."

"That's criminal, man. Fucking dangerous. You can't let that happen."

"What am I supposed to do? Call the cops?"

"Throw her ass out."

I laughed dispiritedly. "You know I can't do that."

"Why not?"

"It's her house too."

"Is it?"

I thought about it. "Well, I was the one who signed the papers and made the down payment."

Pete just nodded and waited.

"But the kids, man. She's their mother. She's not gonna just up and leave them."

"You never know," he said. "Maybe if you make her the right offer."

"Bribe my wife to leave her own kids? Yeah, right." I was starting to think I'd made a mistake asking Pete for advice. *He doesn't know shit about wives and children*, I thought. "Look, I'd better get the kids back home. Lunchtime, you know." I looked around for Josephine, saw her swinging hand over hand on the playground bars.

"Look, Buddy, you know I love you. But you're killing yourself, man. You can't keep this up. You've got to save your own life. Get rid of her. Whatever you have to do. You know, there is this thing called divorce."

"Yeah, think I've heard of it. But I don't want to get into all that. Anyway, divorce always goes against the father. I'm not gonna take a chance on losing my kids."

"Maybe it doesn't have to work that way. I know some good lawyers, man. I could call them."

I yelled for Joey and waved at her to come back. "Yeah, I'll think on it," I said dismissively and stood up. "See you on Monday, man." I plopped Rosie into her stroller, took Josephine's grubby hand, and started off back to our house.

"Life goes on," Pete called after me. "Don't let her ruin it."

"What's Uncle Pete talking about?" Joey asked me as we moved away.

"He's just being funny," I said, though I knew that was not at all the case.

After

Annie made it easy for me. As we were eating dinner one weeknight (I'd made baked chicken), she blurted it out, "I think I'm going to be taking off for a while."

I put my fork down and looked at her. She seemed even thinner and paler than usual. I knew she was smoking a lot of weed and likely using something heavier. "What does that mean?"

"Bing asked me to go on tour with the band." She kept her head down, staring at the uneaten food on her plate.

"I like Bing," Joey chirped. "He lets me play his guitar."

"You've been taking them over to his place?" I was trying to control the heat rising up my spine.

"You said you didn't want me leaving the kids alone." She shrugged.

"You girls go play in your room," I said.

"But I'm not done eating, Daddy. I want dessert," Joey said.

"Later," I said, more loudly than I intended. Both girls looked like they were about to cry, but got up and left the table, Josephine holding Rosie's hand. I waited till they were gone. "What the hell do you mean you're leaving?"

"You know, the band has this great opportunity. We'll be touring all over the Midwest."

"*We* will? Now you're part of the fucking band?"

"I'm sort of a roadie. And Bing says I have a good voice and that maybe I can sing backup on some of their numbers. I'm excited, Buddy."

"How long are you planning on being gone?"

"I'm not sure. A month, maybe longer. We might pick up some extra gigs."

"And your children? What about them?"

"I thought you liked taking care of them." She poked at her food. "I'm just not very good at the whole mother thing. You can handle it, can't you, Buddy?"

I took a breath and tried to collect my thoughts and tamp down my disdain. I told myself I needed to be smart for once and thought about my conversation with Pete. "You're right, I do like taking care of the kids." I paused to catch my breath and plan my words. "I'll be there for them both as long as I'm alive."

Annie grinned. "I knew you'd understand," she said.

"But before you go, I want one thing." I waited a beat till I had her full attention. "I want us to get a divorce before you leave. That's the only way this can work."

"Well, I wasn't thinking that far ahead." Annie picked

up a piece of the chicken and took a tiny bite. "But, cool, if that's what you want."

"I do. And I don't think either of us needs to get a lawyer and have to contend with all that paperwork and court dates and stuff."

"Yeah, me neither. Who needs the hassle?" she said.

"I can get all the forms we need. This is a no-fault state, so all we have to do is register the divorce. I can handle all that."

"But I'll still get to see the kids, won't I?"

"Whenever you want. But they'll be living with me."

"Well, okay then. I guess that'll be best for everybody. What with me travelling around the country and all. I mean, I could even become famous, Buddy. Who knows?"

"It's the right thing to do," I said, feeling my future come back into focus. "It truly is."

Since I was the one who did the paperwork on our divorce, I made certain that it stated clearly that both children would be in my sole custody. Annie barely bothered to read it before signing. She was anxious, I guess, to get on the road, and probably high.

It was also up to me to explain to the girls that their mom would no longer be living with us. "You'll still see her," I told them, "but Mommy wants to go live another sort of life than the one we have here."

"What's wrong with what we have?" Joey asked. I knew

she would need much more explanation but trusted that would come with time.

"There's nothing wrong with our life, sweetie. Not a single thing."

Annie did try to come back to us after a few months, stating that the band was breaking up. She had a defeated look about her, shoulders slumped. But I'd learned my lesson and was happy with the way things stood and didn't want her back in our lives, which is what I gently told her. She didn't make a fuss; I'll give her credit for that. And not long after she announced that she was moving to West Virginia, where her grandparents lived. I told her she was welcome to visit whenever she wanted.

I think Annie only came back to Seattle four or five times over the next dozen years or so. The girls spoke to her on the phone, though I never did. I no longer felt I had anything I wanted to say or hear from her. I still, all these many years later, feel the same way, and I expect that Ann does also. The girls report that their mother has found religion or God has found her. They tell me she's happy now, settled. I am relieved to hear it.

Josephine and Rosie have grown to be fine young women. I'm very proud of both of them, insanely so. Which is not to say the road has not been without some major bumps. Teenage years were particularly difficult. Joey had a serious wild-child period, and Rosie did not speak to me at all for a painful year-long period. Now, we've pretty much worked it all out and are as close as ever. All of us had lots of growing up to do.

As for me, I'm retired now after many years of high-school teaching. It was a good career, just right for me. I feel lucky to have found it. Never did get re-married, though I've had my share of semi-serious relationships. I was never able to fully trust the idea of marriage again. Maybe I just didn't trust myself. But I'm happy living on my own now. Pete and I still hang out. We've taken up fly fishing, and travel all over the West, looking for beautiful places to cast our flies. Sometimes we even catch a fish.

I often wonder if I'd do anything differently if I had it all to do over again, and always come up with the same answer: I wouldn't. I mean one thing follows another. If I hadn't met and married Annie, there would have been no Josephine and no Rosie. And I can't imagine a life without them. If you ask me who I am, the answer at the top of my list is, and always will be—a father.

The Walking Woman

I see the walking woman every morning. She's on the lake path, head up straight, striding along, arms pumping like pistons. It's like she's driving a truck, like she is the truck. I am out this early with my dog, a three-year old Alaskan malamute. I have to walk him before I go to work or else he'll go crazy and tear up the house when I leave. The walking woman wears those big, old-fashioned headphones. And she never looks at me as we pass. She doesn't turn her head away, she just doesn't seem to notice me. Sometimes she will glance briefly at Manny, the dog.

I make up that the walking woman is running away from something. That if she stops, what she is hiding from will catch her. In this way, I make her like me. My first guess is addiction—of some sort. She is trying to stay clean by substituting hard exercise for her shaming weakness. I know about this. You hold on so tight to your feelings that you want to scream, and sometimes you do. But then even that doesn't help, so you have to start moving.

But I drop that fantasy. It doesn't quite fit around her. She's a big woman, five-eleven maybe. I can tell because I am six feet tall myself. And the walking woman is wide at the shoulders and has wiry black hair massed above the sweatband she wears around her forehead. I don't say that she's especially attractive and I don't say that she's not. I think she probably doesn't care one way or the other what she looks like. She stares straight ahead. The walking woman stops only for litter—candy wrappers and paper bags from fast-food places. She picks these things up and carries them to the trash bins.

My second guess is a failed relationship. I know about these also. When I got divorced after eight years with the same woman I didn't know up from down. I was unmoored, floating around like an abandoned boat. If I hadn't had a job to go to, I would have sunk to the bottom. Not that divorce was the wrong thing to do. I came out the other end eventually. And, in a way, I think I'm better off being alone. Human relationships are just too damn hard. A person is better off with a dog. A dog will never turn on you as long as you keep it fed and take it out for walks. A dog will never want to discuss your relationship or try to change you. Dogs do not get their feelings hurt. When you come home from a hard day out in the world, a dog will shower you with unrestrained love. That's what a dog will do.

"Get a dog!" That's what I want to say to the woman

who walks around the lake. "Then you won't have to move so fast or look this angry." But, shit, who am I to give advice? The thing is, though, I do want to talk to her. After all, we see each other now on a regular basis. Every morning at six o'clock. Manny needs to get going at that hour. I don't. Sometimes I can barely keep my eyes open. Especially when I've had a few beers the night before. Manny hauls me around Lake Washington like he is pulling horsemeat on a sled. The lights of automobiles crossing the floating bridge are a live thing, like a snake. Something about this hour makes me sad. When the walking woman approaches with her long strides, I move out of her way. As she passes, I can hear very faintly the music from her headphones—Bach? Manny lifts his head to sniff, decides she is not another dog, and turns away. I sniff too. There is the vaguest trace of perfume. Or maybe shampoo, something floral. Like my ex used to wear. In the moment I feel less lonely.

Today she wears a hat. This is something new. It's a white canvas hat with a brim that folds down and keeps the rain off. I'm happy that she wears it, pleased that she is taking care of herself. The walking woman is in full strut today, head held high, back stiff like an oak rod. I realize that I've made her into an angry person and that this is not fair. "Maybe we're wrong about her," I say to Manny. "Maybe she's only shy, or scared." Manny keeps pulling ahead, his nose snuffling through the wet grass. He's looking for a good place to shit. This is another quality I like about dogs. They are not complex creatures. Dogs are totally pleased with a good place to move their bowels.

I will say hello today. The white hat softens her image. She looks approachable, like an old aunt I haven't seen for a few years. When she is only a hundred feet away, Manny decides he has found the ideal spot and squats on his haunches. At first, I try to pull him away, make him wait until I can speak to the walking woman. But there is no stopping a ninety-pound malamute once he's found the right patch of ground. Damn, I'm feeling embarrassed, turn away from the path. When the woman is only ten feet away, Manny deposits the last of his morning's breakfast. Steam rises from the mound into the dark sky. The walking woman stops.

"You are going to clean that up," she says. It is not a question. She puts her hands on her hips and waits.

I am stunned by her speaking, her strangely deep voice. "I don't have one of those bags," is all I can manage.

"So you were going to leave it here, right? And someone is going to come along and step in it and you don't care."

"Well, that's not exactly how I was thinking about it." I look for a smile, but there is none. She no longer looks like my kindly aunt. Now she is that guy in a bar who wants to punch you in the face. "I'll come back later and clean it up." I want to get out of there but can't seem to get my legs moving. I feel like a student in the principal's office waiting to be dismissed. Or like I'm once again struggling through a failing relationship, unable to come up with the right words. "I have to get going," I mutter. "Work, you know." Manny sniffs at her hand. She doesn't pull away.

"You need to clean your dog's mess up before you go anywhere." Her voice resounds in the surrounding silence. I'm a little bit scared. She reaches into the back pocket of her sweatpants and pulls out a plastic baggie, which she holds out to me. "You should come prepared."

I reach out and take the baggie from her, realizing in the moment that I am now actually speaking with the walking woman. Peculiar as it is, this is what I've wanted all along. We are having a human exchange. "But how am I supposed to get all that in this little bag?" I glance at the prodigious pile of shit. Manny pulls at his leash. He wants to get moving. I rub his head. "Good boy, Manny, good boy."

"So?" The walking woman is staring at me.

"So?" I shrug my shoulders.

"Clean it up."

"Are you planning to wait here until I do?"

She doesn't answer or move.

My eyes move from her to the pile of crap, then back to her. "Look, I can't do it. Sorry, but I really can't. I don't like to be pushed. It's a fault, I know. And you're not my shrink. But there it is. Like I said, I'll try to come back later, that's the best I can give you." I hand the empty baggie back to her.

"Where do you come from, man?" She grabs the bag out of my hand, picks up a nearby stick of wood. "You don't deserve to own this animal." She bends down and uses the stick to scrape the poop into the big-enough baggie, then hands it to me. I don't dare not take it. "I think you can manage it from here." She stoops down and wipes her palms in the wet grass. I hold the bag full of shit at arm's length in front of me.

"I'm originally from Philadelphia," I say to her.

"What are you talking about?"

"You asked me where I was from."

She cocks her head, as if she's seeing me for the first time. "Look, you can't own a dog if you're not willing to clean up after it." She puts her headphones back on, gives me one last hard look, then pushes off into her power walk.

"It's not that simple," I call after her. But she doesn't turn back. I stand there and watch her move away into the pink morning light. When she is almost out of sight, she raises her right hand over her head. It's not a wave exactly, and maybe her middle finger is raised. She doesn't turn around, but I am pretty sure the gesture is meant for me. "Yes," I shout. "Good-bye." Then I drop the bag of shit behind a tree and follow Manny down the path.

One Foot After the Other

A solitary turnip is boiling on the campfire. He had grabbed it along with a dozen eggs and a six-pack before his hasty departure. Buddy has never eaten a turnip before. But that is to be dinner tonight. And he looks forward to it. Now he pokes at the bulbous white root with a stick he's whittled down, feeling like the woodsman he knows he's not. The turnip is still hard, even though it's been boiling for twenty minutes already. He has salt in the camper kitchen. That will help.

He could have gotten other food at the convenience store in Forks, the small town he had passed on the way. Could even drive there now. But Buddy doesn't want to move, doesn't want to see other people. He's alone out here in his pickup camper, parked in a hidden spot above the Pacific Ocean. A turnip, soft or hard, is all he needs.

Buddy has left his wife and two kids behind in Seattle. Told Jenny that he needed to "clear my head."

"Clear it of what?" she'd asked.

"Everything," Buddy said. "All of this." He gestured at their backyard, where their two daughters were playing in the dirt. "Not the kids, I didn't mean that."

"Then what?"

"I don't know," he admitted. "I truly don't know. But I've got to sit with myself and figure it out. Too much city maybe, too much noise. I'm not thinking straight anymore."

"Go then."

"You don't mind?"

"I'm a big girl." She laughed.

Buddy drew her into his arms, held on, then walked into the house and began to pack.

Buddy heads magnetically to the Pacific Coast, to a place he's taken the family camping before. He's always loved the ocean. It soothes him in a way nothing else can. Certainly not the pills, that he's thrown away before heading out. They just dull things, dull life. He cannot bear that anymore. He'll be forty years old in a week. It feels like a storm approaching. Buddy is disappointed in himself. Thinks he should have accomplished more by this point in his life, like many of his friends have. Forty feels unbearable. He knows he should be grateful for all the good things in his life and enumerates them once again now. At the top of the list is Jenny and the kids. *Where would I be without them?* Then he is grateful for other family and friends. For nature in all its ridiculous glory. And enough money, for now, to live a comfortable life. And, he supposes, he must be grateful for the teaching job that pays for all of it, and which is okay, even enjoyable at times. But hardly all that he wants. Back in high school Buddy was sure that someday he would be famous. He couldn't have said exactly at what he would excel, only that he would. He'd have his moment. That moment has never come.

Buddy and his therapist have talked many times about this unfortunate habit of mind, of Buddy's tendency to see the glass half-empty. A metaphor Buddy is not fond of and in his last session told Gerald as much. "It's not half-full or half-empty. It's just a glass of water. I'm not fucking measuring it."

"I think maybe you are," the therapist responded.

Buddy adds some split wood to the campfire, then sets up a folding chair next to the flames where he can observe the bubbling pot. He opens a can of cold beer. "Life is good," he says out loud. And immediately doubts the thought. He looks in the pot again. "Fuck it," he says. "I'm eating you now." And goes into the camper to dig up a plate and a fork. It's going to be a lovely dinner, he thinks. And feels a sweet relief settle in. The boiled turnip is not half-bad, though a bit bland. A steak would have been better.

Later, after full darkness has descended, Buddy reads the one book he has brought along: *Zen and the Art of Motorcycle Maintenance*. It is a book he has read before, yet never fully understood. He sensed, though, it was telling him something important. Buddy doesn't own a motorcycle himself but doesn't think that matters. He's not even entirely sure what Zen is, though he, at Gerald's advice, is now doing a daily meditation session. His mind constantly wanders into the past and future during these sessions, yet there are still moments, only moments, when Buddy feels that he gets it.

After only a few pages, he places the battered paperback aside and gets ready for bed. There's a bunk that juts out above the truck's cab where he nestles into his down sleeping bag. He sleeps soundly, and wakes refreshed; something that rarely happens back in the city. There had been a dream that still fuzzes around his brain. The dream had been pleasant and in it he was young and happy. There was a woman also, a mix of the few women he has loved, and what else? Something sexual. The details are melting away even as he tries to hold on to them and keep them about for another second. "Coffee," Buddy says to the empty camper. "I want coffee."

While the water works to a boil on the camper stove, Buddy decides that today he will walk along the beach. A long walk is what he needs. The early morning air is frigid, and Buddy wishes he had bought warmer clothes. He needs Jenny to remind him of such things.

After two cups of strong black coffee and three fried eggs, Buddy is ready to set out. He pulls on the denim jacket that he has owned since college. It brings him comfort, but not much warmth. He walks down a rock-strewn cliff to the beach, breathes in the salt air of the Pacific, and feels content. This *is* what he needs. The coast here on the northern tip of Washington State is rocky and wild, the rainforest. So unlike the beaches of his youth back in New Jersey, where the hot summer sands were packed with families and beach umbrellas and the Good Humor man ringing the bells on his ice-cream truck. Here there is no sound other than the breaking waves and the wind. No people. None at all. *A blessing?* Buddy shies from the word.

He picks his way along the beach, looking alternately at the breaking waves and down at the hard-packed sand in front of him, watching for the odd shell or agate, maybe a piece of milky beach glass, like his mother used to collect. "Treasures." That's what his mom called all her beach finds. Up ahead he spots a brightly colored object of some sort, stranded on the high rocks. He picks up his pace, thinking this might be a find. As he comes closer, Buddy sees that the round red object is likely a float, from a fishing boat or crabber. He is delighted, imagines showing his beachcombing off to Jenny, who will pretend to be excited about it. But first, he must pick his way up through the boulders to get to the red float. He is only a few steps away from claiming his treasure, when his foot slips into a gap, and immediately Buddy goes down in excruciating pain, and in that moment, he knows both that his ankle is badly hurt, and that it is unlikely anyone will appear to help him.

Tears come to his eyes from the pain. “Goddamn it,” he shouts into the breeze. “Shit, shit, shit.” He is able to sit up, but then discovers that not only has he sprained his left ankle, but also that he cannot extricate the damaged foot from the encircling rocks. Each time he pulls on the foot a searing pain shoots through his body, like someone has touched him with an electric cattle prod. Buddy tries to still his ragged breathing. *Deep breaths, in and out, in and out. I am here. I am here.* His breath slows, he feels a sense of, if not calm, at least, clarity. “What am I gonna do now?” he asks himself or God or whoever the fuck. Maybe this is why he is out here. A test? He tries again to pull his foot loose but is overwhelmed with pain. An ex-basketball player, Buddy has sprained his ankles many times before, and has broken bones and torn ligaments. He knows the pain will subside after a time. Till then he will sit and wait, maybe when the swelling goes down, he will be able to pull his foot free.

A thought comes to him then that sends a blitz of hope and anxiety through his fast-pumping heart. He slaps at the pockets of his jeans, then frantically at the jeans jacket. “Fuck!” He settles down in despair, then shouts again. “Fuck!” Buddy has left his phone back at the campsite.

He reaches again into his right-hand pocket, just to make sure. No phone still, but his hand closes around the pocketknife that he always carries. This opens a moment of hope, though he has no idea how the little Swiss Army knife will be able to get him out of these crushing rocks and do it before the tide comes in and covers his dumb ass over. Visions of that movie, whose title he can't remember flashes through his brain. *The one where the guy gets trapped, and finally cuts his arm off to escape. I think it was his arm, not his leg. I'm not gonna cut my fucking leg off, not with a pen knife.*

All Buddy can do now is wait. But wait for what? The tide? A passerby? He does not want to die. That much is clear now, though there have been times in the recent past, when he considered ending his own life. Had even decided how he might do it, which, ironically, involved swimming out into the ocean, deep and far enough from shore that there would be no getting back. He's realizing now, as he sits in pain and waits for whatever happens next, that death is not at all what he wants. What he wants is to see Jennifer and the kids again, wants that more than he's ever wanted anything. It gives him strength to think about them, to realize that he must keep living—for them, not for himself, and that all his depressions and complaints, and even despair amount to nothing but idle words. The next breath and the one after that are all that matter.

With new determination, Buddy examines the situation in front of him. *There's a logical way to fix this. There must be.* He stares intently at the two boulders that are trapping his foot. He tugs once again, but the foot is so twisted, that every movement only exacerbates both the pain and the constriction. He tries to move one of the rocks, first with his hands pushing against it, but it is too big and deeply embedded. It moves not a millimeter. Then he remembers the pocketknife and decides to try to cut away the sneaker on his damaged foot. He's kept the knife blade sharp and is able to saw through the back portion of the shoe and cut the laces. Now, he figures, when he pulls again, the shoe will slip off. Buddy lies back, and braces his right foot against the opposing stone, which is not quite as large as the other. He focuses all his strength and energy into that foot and sends everything he can muster into one mighty push. Nothing moves, but Buddy will not give in, will not stop. "Come, come, come, come, come," he yells, screams, and then, it moves. Not much. An inch, maybe two, but *it moved, goddammit. It fucking moved.* He takes a breath, and tries again, that same two inches are there. He can rock it back and forth, and he does. Once, twice, again and again. Buddy keeps at it, and now the boulder has definitely loosened, there is slack around the stuck foot, when the heavy rock moves away. He knows what he must do, knows it will hurt. On the next series he must pull his left foot out at the same moment that the boulder moves away. It's all a matter of timing. "Do it, man, do it now!" he tells himself and pushes hard on the rock and pulls with all his might on his left leg. Tears come to his eyes from the pain, but he doesn't stop and then—out it comes in a burst of intense pain and pleasure. Buddy falls on to his back and allows himself to cry.

His relief, though, is short-lived. Buddy wonders if he is able to walk, to make his way off of these rocks and back to his campsite. He glances at the ocean, which has now moved to the base of the stone jetty. *High tide coming.* He tries to stand up. Knows he must. And does, putting as much weight on his good leg as possible. The ankle is now so swollen that it bulges like a water balloon. At least the shoe is no longer there to torture him. The pain is too much, and Buddy sits back down. He looks around him, tries to come up with a plan. He sees once again the red fisherman's float, and for a brief moment thinks that he still wants to bring it home. The thought makes him laugh. *You are a ridiculous man.* But near the float he sees a long staff of driftwood wedged into the rocks. He crawls on his knees toward the stick and is able to pry it loose. "Thank God," he says. Using the waterlogged staff as a crutch, Buddy is able to hop down the incline, keeping the swollen ankle lifted up. The pain has muted now, only a dull, throbbing ache. He thinks he can make it.

He will struggle back to camp. He will not die on the rocks. He will see his wife and children again. Soon. *One foot after the other, one foot after the other.* Buddy knows two things for sure now: life is definitely worth living, and he will never again eat a damn turnip.

The Yellow Cat

The yellow cat leapt up on the table and looked around. I hated that damn cat. I'd inherited it from my friend, Eric, when he moved to Wisconsin. He said that the cat was not a good traveler but wouldn't be any trouble at all. "He knows how to take care of himself," Eric said. "All you have to do is feed him."

I didn't feel like I could say no. Eric was a good friend, and I knew he was concerned about the cat. "What's its name?"

"Guinness," Eric said, "Like the beer."

"Why that?"

"I dunno. Just a name, man."

"Yeah," I said.

"I've got a plant you can have too."

"Whatever," I said.

Ever since, Guinness and I have had an unhealthy and wary relationship. He keeps his distance and so do I. I'm actually a little scared of him. Once I tried to pick him up, and he raked his claws deep down my arm. Now he's just looking for someplace warm to crash out. That's what he does best. Fucking Guinness. I've thought about taking the cat somewhere in the car a long way away and leaving him, but what would I tell Eric? And anyway, Guinness would never let me get him in the car.

But the cat is not what this story is about anyway. Maybe if I had been a different sort of person, Guinness and I would have gotten along better, but I am what I am, with all due respect to Popeye the sailor man. The story is about the girl who lived across the street. Isn't it always? She was thin and pretty and younger by 20 years. She had been very friendly right from the time I had moved into this SE Portland neighborhood, knocking on my door to introduce herself, which I thought was pretty cool, and not something I had experienced before. In other places I'd lived, the neighbors all ignored each other until they had a problem—somebody's dog was barking too loud or they wanted you to take in their newspaper because they were going on vacation. Shit like that. She said her name was Suzanne, but I could call her Suzie. I couldn't stop smiling, until I realized I wasn't saying anything and that this girl probably thought I was mentally deficient. "Uh, well thanks," I got out, apropos of nothing.

"Well, if you ever need anything just let me know," Suzie said, and pointed at the big white three-story house across the street. "I live there."

"All by yourself?"

"No." She laughed. "Just on the first floor. My sister and brother live upstairs."

"All in the family, huh?"

"I guess," she said, probably missing the reference. She was too young. But not really a girl as I first thought. Up close, I could see a slight darkness under her eyes, and a stooping of the shoulders (she was kind of tall). In her thirties, I reconfigured. Still a few years too young for me, if you play by those rules.

She turned to leave, then looked back over her shoulder. "We should go for a walk some time. That is, if you want."

"Definitely," I said. "I'd like that. You can show me the neighborhood."

"I can show you lots of things," Suzie said, and ran down the steps and back across the street to the white house. I watched her all the way. Even as she opened her front door, when she stopped and looked back across at me and waved, like she knew for certain I'd be still watching. Damn, this could be something, I thought and went back into my house, which I now realized was exactly the right place for me.

So, we started dating, though I avoided using that word. I'd been married before and had told myself that I was through with women, or at least with BIG relationships. I just wanted to relax and be by myself and have some sort of simple life, where I did my own cooking and cleaning and shopping at Trader Joe's for the kind of food that I wanted. I thought I was in a good frame of mind, one that I hadn't been in for the previous three years when I had moved to Seattle, to be with another woman and the whole thing turned out to be a major fucking disaster, that left me heaved up on the shores of Lake Union in a shitty little basement apartment where I cooked on a hot plate and washed dishes in the garage and cursed the woman who had already moved on and made it clear that, as far as she was concerned, I could rot in hell.

I'd paid my dues I thought and was really pleased with my circumstances now, having found a good teaching job in Portland and able to buy this house that had three bedrooms and two baths that were all for me. I didn't now want to think of myself as "dating." That would have been too dangerous. What I told myself I was doing with Suzie across the street was "hanging out." Sure.

The relationship progressed pretty quickly. I mean, on our first real date, a dinner and a movie, we came back to my house and had sex. That's fast, man. At least it was for me. I wasn't sure about Suzie. It was all pretty exciting, and I'll admit, I felt swept away, caught up in a tide I didn't see moving in. This was something else, something raw and physical and crazy. I wanted more—and more. It seemed a blessing that Suzie lived right across the street. Damn, I could see right into her front window from mine. Walk across the street anytime I took a notion to. It never occurred to me that at some point this proximity might be a problem, even a cause of pain. I was too happy for that kind of negative thinking.

Unlike me, Suzy was a "cat person." She had five of them. And treated them all like special children. I played along, even pretended that Guinness was an important part of my life. When Suzy was over at my place, Guinness would jump right up on her lap and start purring. Also, Suzy made her living as a Tarot card reader. Seriously. I had always thought of that kind of thing as superstitious at best, a scam at worst. What now to make of a girlfriend who has a business card that labels her as a medium and a psychic. I should have started running, but in my state of constant arousal and dumbass bliss, I pushed all that aside. Next thing I knew I was thinking about asking her to marry me.

And then I did just that. And Suzy looked at me like I'd asked her to spin around on the top of her head and count to thirty. "Why would we want to get married?" she asked. "Aren't we having fun just the way things are?"

"Yeah, I guess," I said, "I just thought . . ."

"What?"

"I thought you might want that," I stammered. "I mean, you've never been married, have you?"

"Oh, I get it," Suzy said, her eyes lighting up. "You're trying to rescue me from my pathetic spinsterhood."

"Withdrawn," I said then, realizing my mistake. "Forget

I said anything. I didn't mean to insult you."

"You're forgiven, old man," she said, smiling again. "Let's talk later." She walked back across the street.

When I went back into my place, Guinness was sitting right there in the living room, like he'd been waiting for me. I swear that damn cat had a grin on his face. Later I called Suzy to see if she wanted to go out to dinner. Maybe we'd share a bottle of wine and she would stay the night. But she didn't return my call. Not then or the next day either, when I saw her walking down the street with some guy I didn't recognize. He looked young.

Buddy The Fool

1.

Buddy grew up in a household dominated by women: three older sisters, an enfeebled grandmother (Bubba), and most importantly his mother—Bertha, a name he would never dare use to address her. Not even after she was very old and infirm. Still, she exerted a powerful force, even in the "extended care facility" where all the nurses were wary of her. His father was also a part of the family, but in a way that obviated his presence. A medical doctor, he tended to his patients and sat in his easy chair reading the *Philadelphia Inquirer* and let the rest of the family swirl about him, with only the occasional outbreak of rage.

Buddy had no comprehension of whether his mother and father loved each other. He never saw them touch, hold hands, have a conversation. How would he know if they even liked each other? Buddy never heard love mentioned in the family circle except in relation to various television shows

(*Milton Berle, I Love Lucy*) or ice-cream flavors (his sisters *loved* rocky road). The parents did not display affection toward any of the four children. In that way, they were consistent. The less talk of a personal nature the better seemed to be the unspoken rule of the family. Dinners were silent affairs. And the food was bland, boiled, and ladled onto a plate with vegetables from a can and make sure you finish every bite. There are people in China who are starving. Buddy dared not ask how they would get his food to the starving people if he didn't eat it. Puzzled by the thought, he tossed and turned in bed thinking about hungry foreign children.

The girls, Buddy's sisters, had more freedom than he did. At least they were more willing to speak up. To, on rare occasions, get away with private jokes and giggles that did not (ever) include their little brother. He was not coddled or fussed over. Rather, they saw him as an irritant, a distraction. If they bothered to think about him at all.

To be clear, Buddy never thought of himself as mistreated or abused. Though, one time when he complained too much about bad dreams keeping him awake, his mother, a large woman, used a curtain rod to convince him to close his eyes. All of which is to say, that Buddy's first true lesson of the world, brought to him by a dominating mother and a slew of angry sisters, was this: Watch your back, boy.

2.

Sex puzzled Buddy. A reasonably popular kid in high school who had gone out on dates, Buddy had never gone beyond second base (over the bra). There had been opportunities, especially with Barb, who he dated all through senior year and had taken to the prom, but when they sat alone in his father's car, borrowed for the big night, and Barb leaned into him for kisses and more, he was scared to go where he wanted to, and she, he later learned, had been deeply disappointed. "I wanted to go all the way with you that night," she told him, laughing, at their twenty-year reunion. Was he shy? Or something more? His sisters only looked at each other and laughed when he asked how to "be with girls."

College years brought more awkwardness and worry, though he did finally get to "go all the way" a few times. None of these encounters were very satisfying beyond his needed release. Buddy thought the girls who allowed him to have sex with them were losers, too unattractive to be with the popular fraternity guys. There was one, a heavy-set Italian girl with a trace of a dark-haired mustache, who called him out on his behavior. After they screwed, in the messy off-campus apartment he shared with three other boys, the whole business taking only minutes, she pulled the soiled sheet up over her body and turned to him, "You're a fucking idiot," she spat.

Buddy was already up and pulling on his pants. He was anxious now to get her out of the house before his roommates returned from their afternoon classes. He was surprised by her words and by the level of anger directed at him. "What did I do?" he murmured.

"You actually don't know, do you?" She sat up, let the sheet slip down to her waist.

"I thought we were just having fun." He couldn't help staring at her pendulous breasts, and despite her very obvious rage, felt a resurgence of lust. "I'm sorry, you know," he said, "if I hurt you."

"You didn't hurt me," the girl, whose name he'd forgotten, told him. "You're not important enough for that. I don't even know why I'm getting mad. This was my mistake."

"What mistake?"

"Fucking somebody who doesn't give a shit about pleasing me."

"You weren't pleased?"

She laughed. Threw the sheet off of her and stood up. "You never even looked at me and you came in one minute."

Buddy was startled, then embarrassed, and the embarrassment turned to anger, all in a moment, and he said, "I didn't know I was being timed."

"Obviously." She dressed quickly. Turned to Buddy before leaving. "Don't you dare tell anyone about this."

"Don't worry," he called after her. "I won't."

After she left, he tried to think about what had transpired and why the girl had wanted him to "look" at her. But not able to come up with an answer, he decided to go have a watery beer at the local townie bar.

3.

He married her because he didn't know what else to do then. And wasn't at all sure he even loved her. No wait, let's be honest here. Buddy, in fact, knew that he did *not* love her, that they had hardly anything in common other than the overriding fact that neither knew what the hell to do with their lives now that they were graduating from college. Her name was Christina, long blonde hair, tall with a slim figure and a conventionally pretty face, very *goyish.* Her Christianity was part of the reason Buddy, a "nice Jewish boy" was initially attracted to her. That and the sense that he was getting a girl he didn't feel he deserved. He knew his parents would disapprove of her and the marriage. Somewhere along the way to independence of a sort, Buddy had quietly disavowed any attachment to Judaism. He hadn't been in a synagogue since his Bar Mitzvah. He now felt ashamed of his Jewishness, his sense of foreignness and his (imagined) ugly Semitic features; had even flirted with the idea of changing his name from Goldberg to Gulden, like the mustard. When the Jewish fraternity on campus had entreated him to join,

Buddy told the upperclassman, who was extolling the joys of fraternal life, that "I don't really think of myself as Jewish."

"Really?" The senior raised his eyebrows. "Why's that?"

"I don't know." Buddy shrugged. "It's all bullshit, really. Isn't it? I mean it's not like we're a tribe anymore. Nobody's out to get us."

"Yeah, right," the senior said. As he walked away, Buddy thought he heard him mutter, "Anti-Semite."

Christina, for her part, also wanted to rebel against her parents' wishes. She had grown up in a traditional Southern white-bread family and felt that her life, up to this point, had been too predictable. She thought it would be "fun" to do something different and bold. In her four years at that small midwestern college, she had been an active member of her sorority, the Chi Omegas, who had a reputation for having the prettiest girls on campus and of being exclusive in choosing members. No Jewish or black girls had yet breached their doors. The sorority did accept one Asian girl, who they managed to feature prominently in every group publicity photo. Certainly none of the "sisters" dated Jewish boys, let alone marry them.

Once they were wed, Buddy and Christina found they had little to talk about with each other and even less desire to do so. They did both enjoy having sex now that they could do it free of guilt and as often as they both liked. Christina was able to teach Buddy about oral sex and how to withhold until she reached an orgasm. He wondered why she was so adept at the assorted variations of the act. Buddy had heard rumors about her back on campus, but decided not to ask about her history and offered no stories of his own.

They moved to the East Coast, where Buddy had been accepted into a graduate program in literature and struggled on for a time. Christina said she wanted to have a career in music, but didn't know quite where to start, especially in this big city where she felt lost and scared most of the time. Buddy worked at various low-paying jobs when he was not in class. For a time, they joined a group of similarly lost couples who smoked pot and talked about sexual liberation. When even that was not enough to hold their interests, Buddy was forced to admit to himself that his parents had been right and Christina was not the right match for him. She was not very intelligent, he thought. Christina wasn't growing, as he imagined he was. It was time to move on, he decided. He wasn't sure where Christina stood and didn't bother to ask.

An experiment gone wrong, that's all this is, Buddy thought, as he packed his bags, readying to move out of their shabby Cambridge apartment. "You know you don't just get to throw me away," is what Christina said then. "It's not that easy!" she added as he closed the door behind him. Buddy was surprised by her outburst, so unlike the complacent Christina he thought he knew, but he kept walking.

4.

A friend turned him on to a vacant, affordable apartment above a bakery near Copley Square. It was the first time that he had lived completely alone. It was a strange feeling to have all this space to himself and to buy his own groceries and even some limited, thrift store furnishings, and to not have to make small talk with anybody and go to sleep alone and Buddy realized he loved this, truly loved it. Why hadn't he figured this out before—that a man was okay without a woman? Buddy determined that he was experiencing "personal growth." He felt fully engaged with the graduate school seminars he was enrolled in, thrilled by the level of academic discourse and the personal connection with brilliant professors and fellow students at the daily afternoon teas. He felt both energized and content—and more than anything, startled that his life had taken this turn. He didn't need Christina in his life. Never had. I am not lonely, Buddy told himself—over and over.

He had almost put Christina out of his thoughts when he returned home one night from his part-time bartending job, to see the blinking red light on his answering machine. Buddy somehow knew immediately it was her. He found himself strangely pleased to hear Christina's voice. She said that she had spent the last eight months in West Virginia and had been actively pursuing a career as a singer and hoped Buddy, "when you have a chance," could call her at the number she left.

"What the fuck." He switched off the machine. What could she want? And did he even want to know? Life was good now, why screw it up? On the other hand, what would it hurt to talk to her, see what she was up to? Maybe he'd call her in the morning. Just to be friendly, you know.

He waited a couple days before making the call. Thought about blowing it off but didn't want to be rude. After all, she'd been his wife, for god's sake. In fact, still was. Neither of them had thought it important enough to bother with divorce proceedings. Maybe she wanted an official settlement. "Fine with me," Buddy said out loud, as he sat in the rear of the lecture hall. A nearby student turned to stare at him. Damn, why am I obsessing over this? he thought, managing to contain the words in his head. "Fucking call her and get it over with." The other student turned around once again, looking aggrieved.

5.

"Hi Buddy," Christina said, "So glad you called back.

"Sure, no problem. Sorry it took so long. I've been really swamped with school and work and all." Buddy thought he could hear a faint strumming sound, maybe just the long-distance connection.

"It's a lot, I'm sure."

"Nothing I can't handle," Buddy said, relaxing somewhat. Maybe she was only calling to check in. Maintain the connection. That's what mature people did.

"So, what I wanted to talk about is . . ." The line went quiet.

"Go ahead. It's all good."

"Okay, then. You won't get mad?"

"Why would I get mad?"

"Well, sometimes you do. At least you did. Maybe all that's changed. I hope so."

"It has." Buddy began to feel a tightening in his gut. "So go ahead and talk already."

"That's what I was afraid of."

"What, dammit?"

"Your temper, Buddy. Your anger."

"I'm not angry, Christina." He took a deep breath, calmed himself. "Say what you want to say. I'm listening."

"I think we need to get that divorce."

"Fine," Buddy said. "No big deal."

"Don't you want to know why?"

"I don't really give a damn, Christina."

"I'm thinking about getting remarried."

Buddy was taken aback. He didn't speak. Couldn't. This was not anything he'd imagined.

"Are you still there?"

"I'm here." He took a deep breath. Buddy felt almost dizzy. "So, when did this happen?"

"I met Harley a couple months ago, at a bluegrass festival. We were both performing. I don't know, Buddy, I guess you could call it love at first sight."

"How nice for you." Buddy could not contain his sarcasm.

"He's a great guy. A little older, you know, mature. And a wonderful guitar picker. We've been playing together lately, all over the state. I think you'd like him, Buddy, I truly do."

"Is he there?" Buddy now identified the background noise as guitar picking.

"Yeah, he is. We were rehearsing."

"Rehearsing, huh? That's cool. Let me talk to him, would you?"

"Why?"

"I don't know. Just want to say hi to this 'great guy.'"

"Don't say anything stupid, Buddy. Please. Promise me that. He's important to me."

"I'm not going to say anything stupid. When have I ever?"

"I'm not going to answer that."

He heard her call out to him, and then a twangy male voice spoke, "Hey there, Buddy. Christina's told me a whole bunch about you."

"Yeah, I'll fucking bet."

"No need for cussing, is there?"

"Don't tell me how to speak, asshole."

"Christina said you might react this way. That's why she's been so hesitant to call you."

"I'm not reacting any way. She's still my wife, you know."

"No, man, she's not. That ended a while ago, and from what I understand you were the one who run off."

"None of your damn business who did what." Buddy felt revved up. "How fucking old are you, anyway, *man*?"

"Well," he drawled, "not that it's really any of your business there, but I'm forty-six years old, hard-earned every one of 'em."

"Jesus, what the fuck does that even mean? You do know Christina's only twenty-three?"

"I do know that. But she's an old soul, Buddy, and a hell of a singer. Two things you probably never bothered to figure out."

"What I 'figure out' is that you're an old sleazebag. And you can tell my wife that there isn't going to be any goddamn divorce." Buddy slammed down the receiver and fell back into his chair. His mind was reeling, unable to form a single coherent thought.

Ten minutes later the phone startled him back to consciousness. It was Christina. "Buddy," she said, speaking deliberately and quickly, "I wanted to let you know that Harley and I will be coming up there to Boston. I'll call you when we get in. We're going to get this figured out. One way or another." Then she hung up.

6.

Buddy had never owned a gun. Jewish guys didn't go hunting; his father had told him that long ago. But now he decided he needed one. The guy behind the counter at the firearms store asked him what he planned to use it for.

"Why's that matter?" Buddy felt nervous as he gazed at the array of handguns displayed in the glass case in front of him.

"All sorts of different weapons, son," the older fellow behind the counter said. "Depends on how you plan to use it."

"I don't plan to use it at all," Buddy said. "I just want to have it around, you know?"

"So, it's for protection?"

"Yeah, right. Something like that."

The man reached below and placed a heavy looking gun in front of him. "This here's a Glock 17. It'll stop a damn elephant in its tracks."

Buddy picked it up and held it in his right hand. He was surprised at how good the weapon felt, almost as if it was a live thing. "I like it, but I was thinking of something smaller."

"Gotcha," the gun seller said. "Here try this one. It's a

9mm compact. You can carry this inside a jacket pocket or in a shoulder holster and nobody will ever notice."

"Wouldn't that be illegal?" Buddy picked up the smaller pistol, admiring the bone handle and gray metal stock.

"Well, you're gonna need a license."

"Is that hard to get?"

"We can do the paperwork right now if you like."

"Let's do it," Buddy agreed, still holding the weapon. "I think this is just what I need."

Buddy's thoughts were swirling, as he walked home. "What the fuck am I doing?" he said out loud. An older woman walking a small dog stared at him and hurried on. "This is insane." Then he thought about his wife and the country singer and kept on walking.

By the time he picked up his new gun and the square box of shells, Buddy had decided what he was going to do. The gun-store owner had shown him how to load the weapon and turn on the safety lock so that it wouldn't fire accidentally. When he got back to his apartment, he loaded five shells into the chamber and flipped on the safety. He then placed the gun in a drawer in the kitchen. Maybe when they arrived, he'd invite them to sit down for a cup of coffee. "Might as well be a good host," Buddy said. He had only the slightest apprehension of possibly doing something cataclysmically stupid. But it was in the air. "We'll see what we see," he said.

7.

A week passed before Christina called to announce that she and Harley were in town and would like to come "visit" with him. Buddy told her sure, why not, and gave Christina the address of the bakery. Forty minutes later, there was a knock on his apartment door. "Hey there," he said, opening the door for them. "Come on in." He almost made a theatrical bow but thought better of it.

"Wow, this place is great," Christina said, looking around Buddy's spacious apartment. "You fixed it up nice."

Christina looked good, better than she had when he'd last seen her. She was now wearing her hair in two long braids, and she'd put on a little weight, which she had needed. "Yeah, I was lucky to find it. I like living by myself." He didn't know why he said that, and silently reminded himself to keep it impersonal.

"I think that is just what you needed, Buddy. I'm real happy for you." She smiled prettily.

He almost smiled back at her, but he was not about to be taken in by pleasantries. Too late for that. "So, are you going to introduce me, or what?" He now looked fully at the grizzled man standing behind his wife, standing there with a dumb grin, and a cowboy hat held in his hands. Buddy was pleased to notice that the old man was a couple inches shorter than he was.

"Oh yeah, sorry," Christina quickly spoke, "This is my friend, Harley Stevens."

Even the name grated on him, but when Harley reached out his hand, Buddy shook it, meeting the man's hard grip. Neither spoke.

"How about if we all go sit down? Would that be okay, Buddy?" Christina asked.

"Whatever you want. Let's go in the kitchen," he said. "Get on with it."

"Sounds good to me," the country singer said, grinning. He seemed to be enjoying himself now, like he was at a social gathering.

Once they were seated around the table, Buddy looked across at Christina. She wasn't smiling; she looked somehow older now and serious, more mature, as if the months away had bumped her ahead a few years. He realized then, with a start, that he didn't want to lose her. She was his wife and belonged with him. He tried to block Harley out of his view, though he was sitting close by Christina's shoulder, and now whispering something in her ear. The anger rose up his spine. "Okay, cards on the table," Buddy said. "What are you doing with this bumpkin asshole?"

"Don't you speak like that, boy. You best show some damn respect here."

"Or else what?"

"Or else you and me are gonna have a problem." Harley

sat up straight, squared his substantial shoulders.

"Both of you, stop!" Christina demanded. "You're behaving like a couple of children."

"This ain't going to work out, honey," Harley said, standing up. "Let's just get on out of here. Let the lawyers handle it."

Buddy stood too, and moved toward the drawer where his weapon was waiting. "Why don't you just get the hell out, cowboy? Go find someone your own fucking age to hit on. Christina's staying here. Where she belongs."

"What are you talking about, Buddy?" Christina said. "I thought we were done for. You're the one who wanted it. Remember?"

"Yeah, well I've reconsidered. I think I was too hasty. I think we can work this out, you know. Maybe we've both changed."

"Too dang late for that, don't you think?" Harley interjected.

"This is none of your damn business." Buddy once again moved to position himself near the gun drawer.

"He's right about that, Harley," Christina said. "Sorry, but this is between me and Buddy. Maybe you could go on downstairs and wait."

"I ain't going nowhere," Harley said. "This boy don't look like somebody I can trust to be alone with you."

"Don't call me a boy," Buddy said. He'd had enough of this fool. It was time to make things right.

"Go on," Christina now told the older man. "I don't need anyone to tell me what to do. That's what this here is all about, isn't it? You two fighting over who gets to own me. You both are just simple."

Buddy couldn't believe what he was hearing. Christina had never spoken so forcefully before. It wasn't only the words that shocked him, but her whole demeanor, her confidence. He irrationally wanted to hug her. "Yeah, I'm acting crazy, sorry," he said, and looked over at Harley.

"Reckon she knows what she needs," he said. "I'll go wait in the car, babe."

"I don't like that name, Harley. I'm no one's baby."

"Didn't mean it that way." He shrugged, put his hat on, and headed for the door. "Don't be long."

Buddy slid open the kitchen drawer and stared down at his new 9mm. There was still time. But he knew now he couldn't do it, and watched as Harley closed the door behind him. He slid the drawer shut and felt the anger slip out of his body in a great rush, like a suddenly punctured tire. Buddy sat down again in the kitchen chair and waited for the conversation he would now have with Christina. He didn't know what would happen next, but started with, "I truly am a fucking moron."

"Won't argue with that," she said, the smile returning.

8.

Of course, things never did work out with Christina. She told old Harley to go on back to West Virginia and she'd call him soon to let him know what was going on. She stayed a week with Buddy, and they enjoyed each other's company more than they ever had, though they both agreed that having sex would be a mistake. But at the end of that week, Christina told him that she was leaving again. She wouldn't go back to Harley. "Guess I've already made that mistake," she told Buddy.

"What mistake?"

"Getting married just to say I am."

"Thanks a lot," Buddy said with a grin. He knew she was right. They both had to get on with their lives.

After she left, Buddy cried. It had been many years since he'd allowed himself that. But afterward he felt clean. He took the gun back to the store and sold it back for half the price he'd paid for it. "Not what you wanted?" the owner asked.

"Nope," Buddy said. "Not what I needed."

"Got some nice rifles."

"How about a sling shot?"

"You messing with me now?"

Buddy shrugged. "Sort of."

"You might want to stop being a wise guy," the man said. "It ain't that healthy around here if you know what I mean."

"What, you gonna plug me?" Buddy said, and turned and left the store before the man could respond.

As he walked back to his apartment, Buddy thought he would call Christina to tell her about the incident at the gun store. She'd probably find it amusing. He really thought she would.

Your Life Has Wings

You stare out the window of your basement apartment and watch your dog running back and forth in the snow. You can tell she wants to leap over the tall fence you have built and run free. Upstairs you hear the sound of many heavy footfalls. A group of alternative lifestyle people live up there. Sometimes they beat on tom-toms. One of them, a pasty-faced kid, tells you they are "into Native American spiritualism." You try not to laugh. This is not how you imagined life would be in your early fifties. Truth be told, it has all gone to shit. It's not that you're depressed. That would be too easy a cop-out. You feel sad, but it's your own damn fault, your own poor decisions. You tell yourself to get up and get moving. Easier said than done, but eventually you struggle out of bed and make strong coffee on the hot plate and drink three cups of the bitter brew and choke down a piece of dry toast to settle your stomach.

You moved to Seattle to be with a woman, an old friend from a previous era of your life. For a minute you thought you were in love with her, but you soon discovered it was another reckless attempt to rescue yourself by changing the circumstances, rather than changing yourself. Then you had to tell the woman, only a few months after moving into her apartment, that the whole thing was a mistake, and you were moving out. You were very sorry, you said. She called you weak, "still a little boy," suggested you see a therapist. You didn't argue, just asked if you could take the dog, which you and she had rescued together from the shelter. She said, "Take whatever you want, asshole."

You called your daughter later, looking for solace. "I never liked her anyway," your nineteen-year-old daughter tells you. "She always acted like she was all that. I'm glad you got out of it. Are you going to move back to Portland now?"

"Don't know what the hell I'm going to do. I gave up my teaching job there and sold the house. Nothing much to go back to."

"Sounds like you're feeling sorry for yourself, Dad. Better get over it."

"What about you? You doing okay?" you ask, wanting to shift the subject away from your miserable life.

"Yeah, I'm good. Jenna and I are moving in together. We decided it was time."

"Time for what?"

"To move the relationship along."

"Move it to what?"

"Dad," she says, "Am I going to have to come out to you again?"

You laugh, but it comes out sounding strained. "I kind of thought you were just experimenting."

"Well, the results are in."

"Okay, good, I'm happy for you." You're not at all sure you believe that. You imagined something else for her. For yourself.

"Anyway, I think you'll like Jenna. She's got a great sense of humor."

"I know I will," you tell her, now feeling at a loss for words, afraid to stumble and say something you'll regret. "I'll call again soon."

"Maybe we should wait a while. You know, let things settle out."

"Sure," you say. "No problem."

"Bye, Dad. Love you."

"Love you too." You hang up and start to cry, but snuff it out quickly. You know you have to move now, get out of this stifling apartment. The drumming has begun above. You run a brush over your thinning hair without looking in the mirror. You grab the dog's leash and a heavy jacket and head out. The big pup is ecstatic, and seeing the leash runs in circles around you. She's a beautiful dog, a huskie, full of energy. You feel better as she leaps up and puts her paws on your chest. You walk out onto the street of this residential neighborhood, the huskie straining to go faster. So you run for a block. Fast. You start to breathe again. Feel the slight tinge of hopefulness settle onto your shoulder like a small bird. "What's the plan?" you say out loud. You have gotten into the habit lately of speaking to yourself. "It's time to get straight, man. Figure it out." But nothing concrete comes to mind. Maybe you could ask for your old job back, though you left there without much notice and in the middle of the semester. The dog has found a patch of dirt with a smell she likes and proceeds to roll about in it. You let her. Why not? She knows how to live in the moment. You'll give her a bath when you get back. You start to run again and pull the dog along, even though you are breathing heavily, feeling lightheaded. "I need to start eating better," you tell yourself and decide to go food shopping. That bird is still perched on your shoulder. Tonight you will make a list. You will put one foot in front of the other. Call the old school. It's not a time for false pride. You'll beg if you have to, if it helps. The worst they can do is say no.

"Fifty-two is not so fucking old," you say too loudly as you approach the supermarket. An older woman pulling a shopping cart glances over at you. You smile at her and wave. She actually waves back. "I'm fine," you shout at the woman, as she hurries off. "Really, I am."

An Old Man Surfs

He should have stayed home and read a book or worked on replacing some loose planks in the upper deck. Buddy Foreman should have done anything other than what he did, which was to grab his board and head down to the beach.

"So what?" Buddy muttered to himself as he walked the few blocks to the surf. He wasn't sure what he meant in saying that. "Fuck it," he said louder. But there was no one about to hear. Then the sight and sound of the surf brought all thinking to a halt. And he knew why he was there. He set about waxing his board, pulled on his booties and hood and made his way down the rocky path to the beach. As he'd anticipated, there was no one else in sight. No other surfers to acknowledge. This was Buddy's beach, his place. He'd claimed it over the past eight years. Not that anyone else was challenging him for it. The waves here were usually choppy and small, too many sets of breakers coming in, one on top of the next. It was a constant battle to get beyond the next set, and wearying. There were more consistent spots farther north or south along the coastline, some very popular with the day-trippers who came down from the city only when the sun came out. Buddy was out here every other day, no matter the season or weather. One day in, one day for recovery. He tried to go out a couple hours before high tide, so the waves would be building throughout his time in the water. Some days he waited ten or twenty minutes between good waves, other days, they came one after the other. Only once in the last few years had he been shut out completely. "You just have to be patient," he told his wife, Lilly. "Eventually the waves will come. They always do."

"Is that some sort of philosophy?" she asked, smiling. "A guide for living?"

"It's not a bad one, you know," he replied. Sometimes Lilly would go with him to the beach and walk while he was in the surf. But not today. She had had other plans, and the tide had turned and he wanted in, and so had pulled on his thick neoprene wetsuit in a hurry and was out the door and now wading into the Pacific, watching where the breaks were forming, looking for the sweet spot. Those first steps always contained both excitement and fear. But once he was out there, nothing else mattered, nothing else even registered.

It wasn't until he had made it past the first set of breakers that he realized the waves were bigger than usual. There had been a heavy rain the night before and winds of 20 or 30 miles per hour that had kicked up the surf. Still the waves weren't so big that he couldn't manage, he figured. But also thought, *Don't get hurt, old man.* Buddy accepted that his body was more fragile than it had ever been before, and a hard wipeout could easily break one bone or another or wrench the titanium screws from a recent back surgery. He'd wait for the manageable waves. Though none seemed to fit that description today and he was anxious for a ride. That was the thing about surfing that brought him out here when all good sense said not to. It was the rush, the adrenaline. Buddy wanted that still. "Never too old," he told Lilly more than once.

"Yeah, right. Keep telling yourself that." Lilly laughed and so did Buddy.

But maybe he could manage this big roller surging toward him. He paddled into position and waited for it.

"Here goes!" Buddy yelled, as he felt the force of the big wave catch him up. He looked down the slope of the wave and tried to stay calm and in control as the board slid down the peak. Then he was up and pulling hard to the left to get into the curl. For the next 30 seconds he was at one with the wave, the ocean, his life. Nothing fancy, just a good, long, fast ride that took him 100 yards down the beach. Such a simple transaction. Perfect. He turned out and began paddling back.

The tide was filling out, and with it came the larger swells. *I'd better go in soon,* he thought. "Just one more good one," he said. Buddy liked to talk to himself with no one about except the gulls and pelicans, the occasional seal. “One more and I’m gone.” But nothing much was coming, or when they did, they were breaking away from where he’d set up. He caught a couple weakies, hardly worth the trouble, and thought maybe it was, after all, time to paddle in, go home, take a shower, relax, call it a day. He took one last look at the horizon. And there it was. About thirty yards off, a major gonzo of a wave. It was rising up behind a set of smaller breaks. Buddy paddled into position, wondering if he should go for it or not. But then, like all good days surfing, he forgot about thinking, and swung the board around.

Buddy hadn’t always been a surfer. In fact, he hadn’t taken it up seriously until he was in his sixties, a time when most surfers had already given the sport up for gentler pursuits. He’d surfed as a kid at the Jersey Shore, but then had put such things aside, as life in all its demands and absurdities claimed and hung tightly to his soul. It had been a decent life—nothing special. He tried to do the right thing and forgave himself for those times when he hadn’t. But after all the storm and turbulence of family, jobs, and the pursuit of dreams had passed, Buddy found himself living happily at the Oregon Coast with his beloved second wife, Lilly. Lilly who saw him for who he was—nothing more, nothing less.

He'd always wanted to live by the ocean, always tried to keep it within reaching distance, even well before the surfing bug hit. He ran, he walked, he collected agates, but stayed beside the water instead of going in it. It was too cold, wasn't it? People didn't swim in such waters. In Washington State, where he'd first landed after escaping the East Coast, the beaches were more huge rocks, than sand. People approached that ocean warily, if at all. Buddy had the distinct feeling that he'd lost something along the way. Maybe if he'd gone initially to Southern California, instead of Seattle, he would have rediscovered the joys of riding the waves much sooner. Though he didn't now regret that decision—if indeed it was ever truly a decision. Life seemed to just happen, only somewhat under his control. Free will as opposed to predestination. Ahab and the whale. Which was he?

Now in retirement, Buddy sometimes wondered why he didn't feel more settled, more at peace with his life. Some days were just fine, especially when he could surf. But other times he couldn't rise above the funk that surrounded him as soon as he awoke. There was no logical explanation for the heaviness he felt. He kept it to himself as much as he could. Didn't want to trouble Lilly, who was almost always upbeat. He often looked at her in amazement. How was it possible to be so consistently cheerful? Buddy knew how lucky he was to have such a person in his life, but sometimes her optimism was hard to understand. "Objectively," he told her, "the world is an awful place."

"You're probably right, sweetie," she said and went on with her gardening.

"It's all a matter of bad or good parenting. I mean, that was the deal with Trump, right?"

Lilly looked up from where she squatted on her knees, digging weeds. "Where did that come from?"

"It's what I've been thinking about."

"Trump?"

He shook his head. "I tried to be a better parent to my children than mine were to me. I did that much anyway."

"You were a wonderful parent, honey. Look at how well your daughters turned out."

"Yeah," Buddy mumbled. "Guess so."

Lilly stood up and brushed the dirt off her knees. "Are you okay, Buddy? Is there something we should talk about?"

"No, I'm fine," Buddy said reflexively. "Just having one of my days."

"Why don't you go work in your shop; that always makes you feel better."

"I don't want to work in the shop. What am I supposed to do there, make fucking birdhouses?"

"You could."

"Shit," Buddy said, stretching the word beyond its syllable. "I'm going to go have a nap."

"I'll call you for dinner."

"Fine." He turned to go back in the house, ready to submerge his foul mood in the blackness of sleep, but then stopped. "Hey, honey. Sorry. I'm being an asshole. I'll get over it."

"Go take your nap," Lilly said. "You'll feel better later."

"I love you," Buddy said. And thoroughly meant it.

"Love you too." Lilly smiled, like only she could.

He knew from the first moment that the wave was too big, steep as the side of a cliff, rumbling like a semi truck. Buddy was looking straight down a slide of more than 20 feet. He clutched the rails in fear, forgetting all form, hoping he could somehow slide through, ride the break like he'd done so many times before. But he also knew from experience what a wipeout felt like when it was coming on, and that's where he was in this instant. The wave was not going to let him ride, it was going to smash him down without pity, like a kid with a toy he no longer wanted. It was in that moment before he was driven down that Buddy relaxed. In that long second he felt released from all the darkness and disappointments of this life. He may have even smiled. Buddy was finally at peace.

A Good Feeling

Being older doesn't make this shit any easier, he thought, then walked into the employment office of Natural Foods Inc. His appointment was at eleven a.m., but he'd come early in case there were any more papers he needed to fill out before the interview. Bisbee Blake was always early to appointments—and everything else. He told the young woman behind the reception desk who he was and why he was there, and she smiled at him in a way he very much appreciated, and then she told him to have a seat and Randy would be with him shortly. Randy, she said, not Mr. Meyers. That's the way they did it now, he supposed. Casual. He wasn't sure he'd fit in. But he was here now, and he would wait.

Bisbee sat down and picked up a magazine he wasn't much interested in, but he didn't have time to read past the table of contents before Randy strode into the room, a big guy with a full head of movie-star hair, wearing faded jeans and a flannel shirt. He came right at Bisbee, smiling, hand extended. Bisbee stood quickly to meet the man's charge, held his own palm out. He thought about turning right around and leaving, but he needed this job. Needed it pretty bad.

"Hey there, Biz," Randy boomed. "Nice to meet you. Come on in, come on in. We'll chat in my office." He pulled on Bisbee's arm.

"I go by the full name. Bisbee."

"Gotcha," Randy said, and smiled like he was waiting for the punch line. And when it didn't come, shrugged and led the way back through the door he had burst out of. Randy settled himself behind an ash-colored wood desk and motioned for Bisbee to take the chair opposite. Bisbee was nervous. He was starting to get that bad feeling again, the one that often presaged his anger. Get right with yourself, he told himself. Relax. No big deal.

"So, you want to work for Natural Foods Inc.?" Then the young man smiled, like they were both in on some joke.

"Yeah," Bisbee said. Then added, "I really do."

"Well, good. Very good." He shuffled through the application forms Bisbee vaguely remembered filling out when he had first responded to the help wanted posting. "And what is it you think you could contribute to this organization?"

Bisbee thought about the question, then answered. "Work, man. I'm a hard worker. Been working since I was sixteen years old. Give me a job, any job, and I'll get it done."

"Let me ask you this, Biz, uh, I mean Bisbee, do you ever shop at our stores?"

"Not really. Can't say I do."

"And why's that?"

"Tell you the truth, these stores are too damn expensive for me. I mostly go to the Safeway. Summertime, I grow a lot of my own vegetables. Tomatoes especially."

"We like to think our prices are competitive with the mainstream grocers."

"Okay." Bisbee nodded. No point arguing.

"What kind of name is Bisbee?" Randy asked. "You don't hear that one every day."

"My mom named me after the town—in Arizona. She was born there, always talked about going back one day, but never did."

"Interesting." Randy leaned back in his desk chair, hands behind his head.

"I guess."

"The reason I asked you about shopping in our stores is because I wondered if you were familiar with our line of organic products and with our customer reps?"

"I'm not sure what you mean about the customer rep thing. It's a grocery store, right?"

"That's not a term we use anymore."

"I do," Bisbee said. "Always have."

"Yes, well perhaps it's an age thing. Natural Foods is an all-purpose facility, a lifestyle choice. People shop here because it's fun, an experience. Our reps are our contacts with the larger community, and as such we want them to be tuned in to the concerns of that demographic. It's all about choices, about organic in the largest sense of that word." Randy paused to let all that sink in, then asked. "How old did you say you were, Bisbee?"

"Fifty-seven."

"Okay, good," Randy said. "That's a good age. Lots of life experience."

"It is what it is. Not much I can do about it."

"Perhaps you could tell me a little about your last employment."

"You mean where I worked?"

"Exactly."

"I did delivery work. For the hospital. A bunch of them actually. Carried supplies between all the different branches. Then I got laid off. 'Staffing cutbacks,' they called it."

"And what would you say was your favorite thing about that job?"

Bisbee laughed, couldn't help himself. "Look, Mr. Meyers. . ."

"Please, call me Randy. We don't stand on formality at Natural."

"Okay, Randy." He paused to think about what to say. "That last job, you know, it was just a job. Something I did because I needed a paycheck. And I did it fucking well. Excuse my French. I've worked hard all my life. Always given a full-day's work for my pay. But to tell you the god's honest truth, I wasn't too excited about any of them. Like my old man used to say, 'That's why they call it work.'"

"What did he mean?" Randy looked at him with a half-smile.

Bisbee shrugged. "It was just a saying."

"Well, good. I think I get it." Randy arranged the papers on his desk. "I believe I've got all the information I need." He stood up and moved around the desk, stood there waiting for Bisbee to stand also.

But Bisbee stayed in his chair and looked up at the grinning young man. "So, do I get the job?"

"We have a lot of applicants to sort through. I've got interviews scheduled all day." Randy shrugged his shoulders.

Bisbee stood. "Probably not, then."

"You can call Shawna later today."

"Shawna?"

"The young woman at the reception desk."

"A customer representative?"

"Of a sort." Randy chuckled, getting the joke.

"A man's gotta eat," Bisbee said. "Gotta pay the rent."

"I know it's hard out there these days," Randy said.

"Yeah, right." Bisbee held back his mounting anger. "I appreciate your time, Mr. Meyers." He held out his hand.

"Thanks for coming in." They shook hands and Bisbee turned and left the office.

Bisbee didn't know what to do with the rest of his day. He could go back to his apartment and read or watch the television, but that would inevitably lead to feeling lonely and disappointed with his life. What he needed now was to talk to a buddy. Tell him or her about that jerk-off Randy. Have a good laugh, hear another voice, someone to remind him that he existed. Only problem was that no one came to mind. Who was there in this city, on a Tuesday afternoon, he could phone up and say, hey, what's happening? Want to get a beer? Used to be lots of people like that. A whole gang and they all knew his name, like in that *Cheers* ditty. But he'd lost touch. People had moved away. Arguments happened. Friends left; they always did.

Since home was out and pals a non-starter, Bisbee kept on walking. One foot in front of the other and repeat. He soon found himself crossing the Sellwood Bridge, stopping midway to look down at the scattering of fishing boats, plugging away. "Looks like everyone is disappointed," he said out loud, though there was no one there to hear him, only the sound of cars whizzing by. Earlier in the year, a young mother had thrown her two little children off the tall bridge in the middle of the night. A guy who lived in a houseboat underneath heard them yelling, but the children were gone by the time he got to them. At least that's what *The Oregonian* reported. Bisbee thought he understood what had made the mother do such a desperate thing.

There was a nice walking path on the west side of the bridge. It led down along the river and eventually into a neighborhood of old homes that looked like they'd been there on the banks of the Willamette forever. The houses reminded Bisbee of his childhood home in Southern Oregon. He felt both sentimental and jealous at once. At least that's what he thought he felt. He needed to be clearer about his feelings. Maybe nostalgic was the feeling rather than sentimental; envious rather than jealous. He'd once dated a woman, a New Age therapist of some sort, who when Bisbee would say something like "I'm feeling lonely," she'd respond, "Loneliness is not a feeling, it's an absence of focus." Those types of comments eventually drove Bisbee away from the therapist lady. But now he always checked to see if what he thought he was feeling actually qualified. He wished he'd asked the ex-girlfriend for a list of acceptable feelings. Then he remembered that he had done that and she (Melanie was her name) laughed at him and said, "If you need to write them down, you'll never understand." Right now, Bisbee felt like he'd like to live in one of these shingled houses with a pitched roof. Move in and sit there all day watching the goddamned river and smoking a fat cigar. *What kind of feeling is that?* he asked Melanie in his mind. He distinctly heard her say, "Angry. That's what you always feel, Bisbee."

He continued along the path, eventually arriving at a public park with swaths of grass, picnic tables, and a boat ramp where some of the fishermen were wearily ratcheting their boats onto trailers. No fish were in sight. A bicyclist zoomed by on his left, the rider dressed all in black, like a zombie spirit. Bisbee looked for a bench. His knees were aching. He spied one, only slightly damp, that was situated on a broad slope above the river. He was cold and hungry, but not impatient to change his circumstances. "It is what it is what it is," he muttered. He relaxed back into the bench, sighed deeply, and just then heard the chiming in his pocket, puzzling him at first, before he recognized the sound as his seldom ringing cell-phone. The tone became more insistent as he struggled to react and get the darn thing out of his pocket, swipe at the answer bar, and almost shout, "Yeah, hello, hello?"

"I'm calling for Bisbee Blake," a woman's voice said.

"This is Bisbee." He didn't recognize the voice, thought at first it was one of those robo-calls.

"This is Shawna from Natural Foods Inc."

"Oh, hi, howya doing?" Bisbee said, awkward now.

She laughed lightly. "I'm fine. Randy asked me to give you a call."

"So fast? Bad news travels that way, I've heard."

"I'm not sure what you mean."

"It's nothing." He glanced at the river and waited, held his breath without realizing it.

"Randy asked me to find out if you were interested in entering our training program. It's a two-week commitment, after which, if everything works out, the company decides where to place you."

"Place me? Like in a job, you mean?"

"Yes, exactly. You'll be paid at our beginning hourly rate during training, twenty-one dollars an hour, after that your pay will depend on the particular placement."

"Geez, this is unbelievable."

"It's pretty much the standard pay rate for the industry."

"No, no. The pay is fine. More than fine. I'm just a little shocked is all. Tell you the truth, I didn't think I had a snowball's chance in hell of getting this job."

"Randy was very impressed."

"He was?"

"Yes, definitely. Maybe I shouldn't tell you this, but he said he thought you had a strong work ethic. The kind you don't see too much of these days. Said you even grow your own tomatoes. A direct quote." Shawna laughed.

"Well, old Randy won't be disappointed. I'm gonna work my butt off."

"I'm sure you will. Can you start on Monday? If that's too soon, we could probably delay it for another week."

"Are you kidding? I can start today if you want."

She made that little laugh again. "That won't be necessary. The training class starts Monday at our Northeast location. I'll text you with all the information you'll need."

Bisbee couldn't think of what else to say, so said only, "Thank you, miss."

"You're very welcome, Mr. Blake. This is the part of my job I really like." She hung up before he had a chance to say anything else.

He held the cell phone out, staring at it. Then shoved it back into his front pocket. For another long moment he sat silently, staring at the river. He felt a swelling in his chest and a shortness of breath. He was either having a heart attack or was very damned excited. He decided it was the latter, and after a few deep breaths, jumped up off the bench and punched the air with his fist. "Goddamn, man! Holy shit! I got a job!" He felt like running around in circles, leaping up in the air like a high jumper, rolling around in the grass. But he dialed himself back, saw that there were other people in the park, some who were now glancing his way. "Hey, you know what they call this feeling?" he shouted at a strolling young couple. They pretended to ignore him and kept walking. Bisbee sat back down on the bench and leaned back with his legs out in front of him. This feeling is called happiness, he said to himself. I'm pretty sure of that one. Looks like I get another chance.

Margaret and Her Daughters

Margaret collected junk. Somehow it just accumulated around her: towering stacks of old newspapers, odd sets of dishes, cardboard boxes that nestled one inside the other, appliances that had long since ceased to function, and lamps without shades or bulbs. There were photographs everywhere; some in frames, and some thumbtacked to the walls in odd configurations. Some were images of people Margaret had known long ago, though she didn't recognize them all. She stood now among the clutter and felt confused.

Margaret was expecting a phone call from her daughter, April. Such a lovely young woman. Always so upbeat and friendly. She was supposed to call. Margaret was almost sure of that. But where was the phone? Her daughters had recently bought her a new one. A smartphone, they called it. "It will be more convenient, Mom. You can put it in your pocket and take it wherever you go, even outside in the garden." Margaret didn't think a person should carry a telephone everywhere they went. She rarely used it anyway, and as it had been some time since she had made or received a call, she had absolutely no idea where the darn thing could be. "Oh well," she said out loud. "Oh well."

She hadn't always been so absent-minded, hadn't always felt so sad. *When Rose and April were children, I was different*, she told herself. *They looked up to me. We had fun. I gave them what they needed.* But that image of youth and strength was fuzzy, almost like a dream. Margaret was no longer sure of what had happened back then. She tried now to remember more. *How did I look then? Did I wear hats and stylish dresses? Did the girls hold my hand when we went to the park?* She sighed, even as the questions drifted away. The sound of the chirping phone brought her back. Margaret turned in circles. She could not localize the sound. She lifted a pillow here and a couch cushion there, moved some boxes of *Newsweek* magazines aside, felt she was getting nearer to the sound and waited for the next ring—or whatever the noise that thing made. Why wouldn't they let her keep her old phone? The one that had always hung on the wall in the kitchen. When the unfound phone went quiet, Margaret sat among the couches and tables and dusty rugs, the bones of her life, and began to cry.

April left a message on her mother's phone. She was sure Margaret was at home. Where else would she be? She decided to call her sister, Rose. "Look, I'm worried about Mom. I've been calling over there all day and there's no answer."

"So? She's probably lost the phone. Wouldn't be the first time."

"Nice of you to be so concerned."

"April, this is not a good time. Is there something specific you need from me?"

"Yes, there is."

"And that would be?"

"That you and I go visit Margaret."

"I can't do that. I've got a stack of freshman comps a mile-high sitting on my desk, and carpets in dire need of vacuuming."

"Rose, honey, I'm talking about our mother who may very well be in trouble, and you tell me about your fucking carpets."

"Your language is so unpleasant. Frankly, I'm not at all comfortable when you speak to me like that."

"Oh, fuck that, Rose. I think Mom needs our help, needs us to, you know, intercede. What do they call it?"

"I have no idea."

"When friends step in to help, to save someone. They did it for John Mulaney, that comedian dude. Really funny, brilliant actually, but doing all this coke and ruining his life.

So his friends did an intervention. That's the word. Got him into rehab."

"Does this rambling have some purpose, April? I think you've lost me."

"Wouldn't be the first time."

"We can end this call right now? I don't stand for insults. Not from my students, and not from you."

"Okay, forget it, Rose. Forget the whole damn thing. I'll go myself."

"I didn't say I wouldn't go."

"You didn't?"

"No. I simply don't care to be manipulated. I've had enough of that in my life."

"Got it. I think." April paused, tried to reset. "So, can you meet me over at Mom's? It'll be like old times."

"That's what I'm afraid of. But I suppose it's what's called for."

"Cool. I'll meet you there in a couple hours then?"

"I can hardly wait."

Rose shoved the phone back in her pocket. "Goddammit," she said aloud, then shook her head. "My language is as foul as April's." Like many people who have lived alone for many years, Rose had fallen into the habit of speaking out loud. She found it comforting. At times, she addressed herself to Sinbad, the black cat she had bought as a buffer against loneliness. Unfortunately, the cat didn't understand his intended function and, except for feeding time, did all he could to avoid Rose's attention or touch. She stared at the stack of papers on her desk and shrugged. "Well, I didn't promise I would return them on Monday, did I?"

Rose had a sudden urge to write in her journal. She tried, as her psychologist had recommended, to fill up a page or two every day, but often felt there was nothing to say. "No Whining Allowed," she had noted on the front page of her journal. It often stopped her from writing at all. But the phone call from April had stirred up her thoughts, brought back to mind all the ancient injuries she had suffered at the hands of family, and so she opened the small notebook and wrote: *I do feel somewhat responsible for mother, even worried. The old woman could easily hurt herself. She barely knows where she is most of the time. But when has Margaret ever been concerned about me? Who was there for me when Dad ran off? Dear Mother drove him away and I paid the price. It wasn't Daddy's fault. Who could live with that woman? I'm surprised he lasted as long as he did. Then when he was gone, Margaret never even mentioned him again. It felt like half our life just disappeared. At least mine did. Once Mack left, fled actually, I think I started to hate Mom. I could barely talk to her or her to me. Stumbling around all sweet and confused, expecting the world to feel sorry for because she had two kids to raise on her own. I wasn't buying it, even then. So what? People have to deal with all sorts of hard stuff. I do. Does Margaret think about what my life is like? Did she ever?*

Rose slammed the journal shut. Took a deep "cleansing" breath. Did it again. "Well, I guess it's time to go to Mother's house," she said to no one but Sinbad. "If you can call that hovel a house. Shack is more like it." The cat scampered away. Rose walked into her bedroom. The sunlight was streaming in through the window and for the tiniest moment she felt happy. Was this what they called joy? But then the moment passed, and a great swelling of despair rushed up into her chest.

April was feeling juiced. There was a mission to accomplish. Time to get Margaret straightened away. Of course, she had been on this mission before. Her mother might seem improved for a day or a week, but then would slip back into her daydream world where April could no longer locate her. But she wouldn't think about that now. She gathered up sponges, buckets, a mop and broom, all the cleaning solutions she could find stashed under the kitchen sink, then tied a red bandanna around her untamed black hair. This will be a kick, she thought. The three Morrison women together, shoulder to shoulder against the world. April laughed as she dragged her supplies out the door and into the back of her beat-up old Toyota. She started the motor, hit up Pandora and played Aretha—loudly.

Margaret still sat on the floor, propped up against a faded sofa, when she heard the knock at the front door. An outside observer could have told her that she had been sitting in that exact position for more than two hours, but there was no such observer, and she was no longer a reliable witness to the passage of time. The knocking grew louder. "Oh my," Margaret said and pulled herself up by leaning one elbow on the sofa. The effort took her breath away. She threaded her way through the stacks of folded grocery bags to the front door and began unfastening the complicated lock her daughters had insisted she have installed. When she finally managed to get the door opened, she didn't at first recognize the two women standing on her porch with mops and brooms in hand. Had she called a maid service?

"Ma, hi. Are you okay?" It was her daughter April. She saw that now and allowed herself the breath she had been holding.

But who was this other person? The scowling one. She seemed angry. "It's me, Mom. Rose. Your other daughter. Are you going to invite us in?"

"I know who you are, Rose." She stepped aside and the girls edged past her into the house, dragging their cleaning supplies. "Of course I know my own daughters when I see them," she muttered.

"Mom, we came to clean," April said. "I called you up, but there wasn't any answer, so we just came on over. We'll make a day of it, like old times."

"God," Rose said, "I can't believe what this place looks like. It gets worse every time. How do you even move in here?"

"I really must sit down," Margaret said.

April took her mother's arm. "Sit, Mom. We'll go make tea and then the three of us can chat. Okay?"

"That would be lovely, dear. I'd like that." She sank down onto the couch and let her eyes close.

"Come on, Rose," April said. "Help me make the tea."

"I don't want tea. Assuming we could even find anything in there." Rose nodded in the direction of the kitchen. "Tea is not going to solve the problem in front of us. We have to stop avoiding the issue. Isn't that why we're really here today? You said it yourself. An intervention."

"What is she talking about?" Margaret opened her eyes and looked up into the sour face of her older daughter.

"It's nothing, Ma." April smiled at her mother, then turned to Rose. "Not now, okay?"

"Why not now? When should we do it, April? We're all adults here. When do we get to speak the truth?"

"For fucksake, Rose, we came to help Mom clean, not to have a damn therapy session."

"Well, I believe that's exactly what's called for. We need to clear the air. Say what needs to be said." Rose squared her shoulders. She'd barely moved since entering the house. "This," she gestured at the room and at her mother, "will not be helped by mops and brooms."

Margaret felt her spine stiffen with pain. She didn't understand what her daughters were speaking about. Her heart fluttered in her chest. She felt there was something she needed to say but couldn't find the right words. "When is that man ever going to get home? I can't hold dinner forever," she finally said.

"What man?" April asked. "Who are you talking about, Mom?"

"See?" Rose demanded. "See what I mean?"

"Yeah, I see, Rose. But I don't want to discuss it right now." She glared at her sister.

"Well, I do." Rose deposited herself on the sofa next to her mother. "I've got to process this."

"You're a real shit, Rose. Do you realize that?"

"And you're in avoidance. You do that because you've never come to terms, as I have, with the pain of our childhood."

"Give it a rest, will you? Those therapy sessions are messing with your head."

"Girls," Margaret piped up. "Please don't fight. I thought we were going to have a nice cup of tea. And some cookies, those ones with jelly in the center."

"Sure, Mom," April said. "We'll go look for them right now."

"I wouldn't eat anything I found in this house," Rose said. She turned quickly toward her mother and grabbed her hand.

Margaret tried to pull away, but this woman had a very firm grip. "What do you want?"

"You're scaring her, Rose. Stop it!"

"Mom?" Rose tugged on her mother's arm, trying to bring her closer. Margaret pulled back, but Rose continued. "April and I think it's time for you to move out of this place. Go somewhere, uh, nicer, some place where there are people to look after you, help you with your condition."

"Goddammit, Rose. We didn't talk about this."

"Well, we should have. Isn't it clear she can't cope? Must we wait until we get a call from the police?"

"Shut it, Rose. Right now!"

"What is Rose talking about?" Margaret turned to her youngest. "What do you want me to do?"

"I don't know, Ma." April gazed at her frightened mother. "Maybe we do need to talk about all this."

"Of course we do," Rose said.

"Let me explain it to her."

"Well do it then. And for God's sake, don't sugarcoat it."

Margaret saw that April looked worried but didn't understand why. And Rose, poor Rose, would not let go of her hand. So funny, she thought, how life turns everything on its head. When Rose started in to junior high school, she refused to hold my hand. I guess she's over that now. Maybe we can be friends again. It's nice that they both came to visit. She smiled at her daughters.

"I think what we're trying to say is that . . ." April stopped and cleared her throat. "Maybe it's not such a bad idea for us to think about some other possibilities for you, Mom."

"Possibilities for what, dear?"

"Come on, April. Say it clearly or I will."

April glared at her sister and went on. "Maybe this house is becoming too much for you to take care of, you know. And maybe we could look for s different kind of place for you to live."

"Stop with the maybes. It's called an extended care facility," Rose butted in. "A nursing home. There are some very good ones available. I've been doing some research."

Margaret pulled her hand away, with surprising force. "I don't want that! This is where I live, where I've always lived, and where I want to die when the time comes." Her heart was racing. Why did these girls always demand more from her than she could give? She had tried so hard. Ever since Mack left, each day had been a struggle—to find them the right clothes, to prepare the food they liked, to not be embarrassed by the food stamps she had to use at the market, to not give up. It was not the kind of life she had imagined for herself. There was always something more she had to give up, another painful step she had to take. "Please leave me be, girls. Please."

"Now look what you've done," April said.

"What I've done? God, it must be lovely to go through life never having to confront the truth. You're just like her."

"Go to hell, Rose. You don't know shit about my life."

Margaret stood. "It's time for my nap. I always have a nice nap in the afternoon." She walked away from the two girls and didn't look back.

Two hours later when Margaret came back downstairs, the girls were gone. *What was it they had wanted? Some awful thing about leaving my house.* Maybe it got a bit messy at times, but wasn't that what homes were for? A place you could relax and be yourself. Her ex-husband had more than once accused her of not being able to let anything go. "Clutchy" he had called her. "Clutchy Maggie." She didn't like to think about that and pushed the memory aside. Now what was it she was supposed to do? She sat down in her favorite maple rocking chair, closed her eyes and tried to concentrate, but soon forgot what it was she was trying to remember. When she opened her eyes some time later, she noticed the folded yellow piece of paper sitting on top of the coffee table. She unfolded it and read:

> Dear Mom,
>
> Sorry that we upset you. It's just that we worry about you living here all alone. But it's your decision, no matter what Rose says. She sometimes goes too far if you know what I mean. Please call when you wake up. We want to take you out to dinner.
>
> Love you,
> April

Rose was still upset. She knew that her sister and mother liked each other better than they liked her. "Just because I'm the only one willing to speak the truth, they make me the bad guy. But I am decidedly not that person."

Sinbad arched his back and rubbed up against her leg, anxious to be fed. Rose kicked him away and the cat yowled with irritation. She stamped her foot, and the cat fled the room. "God, look at me. I'm losing my mind." She thought about calling Marya, her therapist. But the last time she had called, Marya seemed irritated, and was short with her.

"We'll work on that in our next session, Rose. For now, try deep breaths."

"I am so tired of all this." She looked around her solitary apartment, at the stack of papers on her desk, at the single still life painting—of a blue vase with three oranges. "Who actually lives here? Who am I?"

Sinbad edged his black head back into Rose's line of sight. The cat was making a mewling sound. He hadn't eaten all day. "Damn irritating animal." Rose reached for the nearest object, a large russet potato, turned and hurled it at the cat. The whole motion was so seamless and unplanned that it caught her by surprise. Rose felt an instant sense of pleasure in her own dexterity—a direct damn hit. Sinbad yowled once and then went quiet, dropped onto his side and lay still.

Rose felt stunned, but strangely not horrified. She nudged the fallen cat with the toe of her shoe. He didn't move, but his black eyes seemed to shift slightly and stare up at her. Sinbad's rib cage moved, though weakly. "Now what would Marya say?" And despite the scene of carnage at her feet, she laughed.

She considered her options. She could drag the cat into that cardboard carrying case she had somewhere and take him to a veterinary clinic. "But what am I to say to a vet? Can you help us? I've just thrown a large potato at my pet." No, there was nothing to do except let the animal expire.

But now Sinbad's rear legs were twitching, and he seemed to be struggling to get up. "This won't do," Rose announced, and walked to the stove and picked up the cast iron skillet that sat on top. I'll need two hands for this, she decided as she moved back toward the shaking cat.

"Fucking Rose," April said. "For a smart woman, she sure acts like an idiot at times."

"Why do you think she's smart?" Kenji asked. "Just because she's a professor, doesn't mean she's got it together. I mean, smart is more than IQ."

"Rose worked really hard to get where she is. It took her almost ten years to get her PhD. She hasn't had an easy life."

"So, now you're defending her." Kenji looked around his girlfriend's apartment. He loved how the place reflected April's usually upbeat nature. Her walls were covered with colorful art works, some of her own, many from her artist friends and acquaintances. The furniture was sparse, but comfortable, and no giant flat screen in sight. That she hid in the bedroom. "I know she's your sister, but from what I can see, the woman is flat-out mean."

"I think she means well. Rose just has a hard time expressing herself in a kind way."

"Maybe because she isn't fucking kind."

"Rose is dealing with a lot of stuff."

"Aren't we all? You can't keep making excuses for her."

"I can if I want." April laughed.

Kenji laughed too. He did love this woman. "Let's go for a walk. I need to stretch my legs."

As they set off down the tree-lined street, their hands slipped together. They strolled in comfortable silence. April felt, for the first time that day, free of all family anxiety. She felt safe with Kenji. He was there for her in so many ways. A "mensch," her father would have said.

"What are you thinking about?" he asked.

"Nothing much. How nice it is to be with you, to be out on a summer evening in the city."

"You know, we could be spending a lot more time together."

"Sure. That would be nice, honey." April watched as a tough-looking yellow cat slipped into an alleyway.

"No, I mean like a whole lot more time."

"Well, I do have a job. But you're always welcome to come watch me in action. I could even get you a free cup of coffee."

"You don't have to be a waitress, you know."

"That's not what my checkbook says. Anyway, I don't mind it. I make decent money, and I get to hear some interesting stories while I work."

"There are a lot of other jobs you could do. You do have a degree as I remember."

"Everybody has a degree in this town. The guy who washes dishes has his master's from Princeton." April stopped and turned to face him. "What are you getting at, Kenj? I like what I'm doing with my life. Most of it, anyway."

"It's just that I worry about you. Always trying to fix your mother and sister's lives. You deserve more." He looked down at his shoes.

"And you're the guy who's going to give it to me." April laughed, a soft sound in the quiet evening.

"I could be. If you'd let me further in."

"I didn't think you could get in any further."

Kenji chuckled. "That's not what I'm talking about." He took a deep breath. "I want us to share a life, to share everything. To be each other's comfort, and joy."

"Sounds kind of heavy."

"I don't mean it to. It's a good thing I'm imagining."

"Yeah, I can see that, babe. I can. I do want to let you all the way in. And I'm getting really close. I just need some more time. You understand, don't you?"

"I can wait," Kenji said. "But not forever."

Margaret was going to have dinner with her girls. April had called to invite her. It was always April who called. She was a good daughter, so helpful and pleasant. Rose was good at heart too—only different. An image of Rose took shape in Margaret's mind—as usual she was frowning. If Mack had stayed around things would have turned out differently. But she hadn't known how to be the woman he wanted. She wasn't smart enough for him. Not that he ever said that in so many words. But after the first couple years, his attention was always somewhere else. And all those people, those friends of his, always around. She should have seen what was coming. When Mack started getting those poems of his published, things changed somehow.

"As soft and coarse as sand," Margaret recited aloud. "She walks in beauty that does not exist in the world." What did all that mean? Mack said it was a poem for her, but she didn't understand why. Those other people were to blame. Writers they claimed to be. Margaret made pots of coffee for them as they filled her house with their foul cigarette smoke and endless chatter. She smiled and smiled until her face hurt, but they never included her in the conversation. All was directed at Mack. He was the hot center of their universe and she a distant satellite. Oh, sometimes her husband would bring her into the mix; catch her up by the waist and swing her about in his exuberance. Then put her down just as quickly, kiss her on the cheek, chant, "Maggie, my Maggie. Sweet girl you are," and return to the dark-visaged poets drinking her coffee.

Even the birth of their first daughter didn't fully claim

his attention. And then Rose had been such a sickly child, always crying. In his own way, Margaret was sure that Mack did love them, but his own way left little space for family.

Margaret sighed and shuffled into the kitchen. She could stand a hot cup of tea. The surface of the stove was covered with lidded pots and frying pans, and even a copy of *Organic Gardening* magazine. "I'd better move that," she told herself. Then she remembered that earlier conversation. She wouldn't let them displace her. "I'd rather have it over with." Margaret moved the magazine and rearranged the pots and pans until she had cleared a spot. She lit the gas burner and placed the kettle on the flame, but by that time her interest in tea had waned and her mind drifted. She gazed out the window. The garden needed weeding and watering. "Tomorrow I must tend to it. I truly must." She continued to stare, focused somewhere beyond what her eyes saw. *It all goes by so fast,* is what Margaret thought. So very fast.

April knocked loudly at the front door for more than a minute, then made her way to the back yard. Through the window she could see her mother standing immobile in the kitchen. She waved but got no response. "Oh shit," she muttered, and rushed to the back door, ready to put her shoulder to it, but the doorknob turned easily. "Mom, are you okay?" April placed her hands on her mother's shoulders and tried to gently turn her around. "What's going on?"

"No!" Margaret snapped. "No, I don't have any more

coffee." She turned to face this woman, this invader in her kitchen. "You people seem to think coffee is the answer to every little thing."

"Mom, what are you talking about? I just got here." Without intending to, she gave her mother a rough shake, then looked around. "Jesus, what the fuck is this?" A black haze covered all of the entryway and the acrid odor of burning metal filled the room. April rushed to the stove, shut off the flame, and, grabbing a dish towel, lifted the blackened tea kettle over to the sink and turned on the cold water. The hissing steam added to the chaos of sounds and smells that her mother seemed unaware of. April pried open the window above the sink and took her mother by the hand and led her out the back door.

The feel of the bright sun warming her skin lifted Margaret's spirit. She came back to the present. "Is it time to leave for dinner, honey? I guess I lost track of myself for a bit there."

"Yeah, you did, Mom. What if I hadn't come by just now?"

"But you did, dear. So there you are."

"There I am."

"Shall we work in the garden a bit?" Margaret moved toward the neatly arranged rows that stretched to the edges of the lush backyard she had created over the years. "I do love it here. Nothing bad ever happens in my garden. Except for the occasional slug I have to drown. I never know quite what to do about the slugs. But I can't let them have all the lettuce, can I?"

"I suppose not, Ma. But I told Rose we'd meet her at the restaurant at six, and Kenji is coming too. Do you remember him, the guy I'm going out with?"

"Of course I do. Nice young man; he looks like your father. He's not a poet, is he?"

"No. Kenji's a tech person. Works for Intel. Makes pretty good money. Stock options, bonuses. All that good stuff."

"Well, he sounds very nice. Very responsible. Not like some men."

"Maybe we should start getting you ready. The smoke is probably cleared by now."

"What do you mean, April? What smoke?"

"Never mind, Mom. Let's find you something pretty to wear."

Two days in a row spent with her mother and sister. How did she let this happen? She and Marya had concluded that this was a situation Rose should avoid. When she was with her family her emotional age dropped immediately to sixteen—or maybe six. "And April is bringing that awful foreign boyfriend of hers. She always has to rub it in. Make it clear to Margaret and the rest of the world which sister is the desirable one." Rose slung open her bedroom closet door. "I suppose I have to wear something acceptable for this charade." What was the point of this dinner anyway? Why couldn't they all admit that Margaret was no longer competent to live on her own? Everyone would be much happier if we put her away—someplace safe, and inexpensive. "I don't have time for this drama." She looked around for Sinbad, thinking to feed him before she left, then remembered what she had done and felt a fleeting moment of shame. In the end, she had wrapped the cat in a plastic trash bag, secured it with a twist tie, and deposited the surprisingly heavy parcel in the dumpster at the rear of her building.

Despite the warmth of the evening, Rose chose a black skirt and a loose black wool sweater. She dressed almost exclusively in black. Found it slimming. Her students, she had discovered in an overheard conversation, referred to her as the Black Maiden. Rose took it as a sign of respect. She checked her appearance in the dresser mirror, combed her short dark hair neatly to the side and took a deep breath. A cleansing breath as Marya referred to it. "I'll have dinner with them, but I'm through playing nice."

Kenji arrived at the restaurant promptly at six and looked

around for April. He was feeling slightly nervous, a little off-balance. He knew family dynamics could be complicated, and he was the outsider here. His sense of unease was heightened by a factor of ten when he spotted Rose sitting alone at a corner table. She glanced his way but made no welcoming gesture. Even at a distance she appeared to be scowling. "Shit," he muttered, and walked across the room. "Hey Rose, how're you doing?" He tried a smile, but felt it quickly collapse under the weight of Rose's stare.

"I'm fine. Why do you ask?"

"Just something to say. You know, like 'How's life'? 'Good to see you.'" He slid into a chair positioned as far away from Rose as the table allowed.

"I never say those sorts of things. Not only are they clichés, but also just another way for people to keep lying to one another."

"Well, I guess we all try to do our best."

"Another cliché," Rose spat.

Kenji picked up the leather-bound menu. He couldn't help smiling. Rose was so over the top. Maybe it was all part of an act, some kind of intellectual posturing. "So, where's my sweetie?"

"Your what?" Rose glared at him.

"My sweetie, your sister."

"Hasn't anyone told you what century this is? Does April know you refer to her in that patronizing way?"

"She calls me the same. Honey, darling. They're terms of endearment, not insults."

"You're trivializing her, trivializing each other. What a ridiculous, saccharine ritual."

"Come on. Are you for real with this?"

"Can't you believe that a woman would speak her mind without apologies? That's not how it works in this country."

"I'm from this country, Rose. Born in Connecticut."

"Whatever." She paused, wondering briefly if she'd misspoke. "I suppose April has told you all sorts of stories about me."

"What was she supposed to tell me?" He looked up from the menu. This was going worse than he imagined.

"Oh, the usual sob story. How I bossed her around when we were kids and took her toys— typical infantile complaints that she's apparently carried into adulthood. Being the older sibling, I always bore the brunt of the blame. And April was always just so innocent. A total act, of course. If you ask me."

"I'm not sure what we're talking about here, Rose. All April told me is that you've had a hard life. She didn't go into any details. But I got the definite impression that she's proud of what you've accomplished. I think she even looks up to you." He put down the menu and looked at the woman across the table and thought he detected a softening in her eyes.

"I don't know how true that can be," Rose said.

"How true what can be?" April asked, smiling broadly.

She and Margaret were standing now by the table alongside a dapper-looking male server, holding more menus. April guided her mother to the seat next to Rose, then bent over and kissed Kenji on the lips and slid into the seat next to him. "So what were you two talking about?"

"It was nothing. Just some small talk. I asked Rose about her teaching."

"I don't need you to lie for me, Kenji. I thought I made that clear."

"Rose always has spoken up for herself," Margaret said. "Even when she was a little bit of a thing."

"Don't infantilize me, Mother. That's what you've always done. It's not nearly so endearing to me as you might think."

"Well, I suppose you have a point, dear," Margaret mumbled. "I'm very sorry."

"It's okay, Mom." April said.

"It's not okay. If it was, I wouldn't have said anything." Rose slammed her menu closed.

"Would you please not start," April said. "Nobody wants to argue with you, Rose."

Rose pushed her chair away from the table and stood up, almost slamming into a server passing behind her.

"Rose, sit down!" April pushed away from the table, but Kenji held her back.

Rose's voice was choked. But no way would she cry in

front of them. "I know you all dislike me. Don't you think I can see that?"

Margaret leaned toward her eldest. "No dear. That's not true. We love you very much."

Rose stepped back and held up a hand. "Don't, Mother. Just don't! You haven't had time for me your entire life, so don't start pretending now. There was always someone more important, someone who needed you more than I did." Rose was almost shouting now, and heads turned toward their table. "First it was our father, and then when you drove him away, it was April who got all the attention. Well, what was wrong with me?"

"I tried to love you, but you pushed me away." Margaret spoke barely above a whisper.

"Oh god," Rose wailed. "I was only a child."

Margaret began to stand, to move toward her daughter, but Rose backed away. "Don't you touch me." She took a deep, ragged breath, and keeping her palm up, backed away from the table. "This was not a good idea. Sorry if I've ruined your little family get-together." She turned and walked quickly away.

Margaret stared straight ahead as April reached over and took her hand. "It's okay, Mom. Rose is going through a rough period right now. I don't think she means half the things she says."

"It's okay," Margaret said. "I understand about pain."

She picked up her menu. "Now what do you think I should order?"

"The roast chicken is good," Kenji said.

"Forget the damn chicken for a minute, Kenj. Maybe Mom wants to talk about Rose."

"What is there to say, dear? Rose is right. My concerns were always with others. Rose came along when it was all I could do to get through a day. She was one of those babies who cry all the time. Colicky, we called it. I could never do anything to settle her down. My whole life felt out of control. No matter what I did, it was the wrong thing. Rose cried and Mack just sat there with his friends and made jokes. 'Take her away, Maggie, won't you? We can hardly hear ourselves think.' It wasn't till I gave birth to you that I was able to smile again."

"Oh Mom."

"But by that time your father was drifting away, and I was terribly upset. I'm afraid poor Rose got lost in the confusion of it all. I've never known how to make it up to her. It's true. I didn't love her enough."

"You did your best, Mom. You must have felt so alone, and so scared."

Margaret pulled her hand away. "I'm still scared. Every day, honey. But what can I do?"

"Maybe we should order now," Kenji interrupted. "I think our waiter is getting antsy."

"He can wait." April moved her chair closer to her mother. "Mom, listen. I have an idea. Do you want to hear it?"

"Well, yes. But I do hope this isn't about what you and your sister were suggesting earlier today."

"No, it's the opposite of that." She turned toward Kenji. "You need to hear this too."

He nodded. "I haven't missed a word yet."

April took a breath. "How would you like it, Mom, if I came back home? If I moved into the house with you?"

Margaret's hand rose to her cheek. "Oh my. I couldn't ask you to do that for me."

"You didn't ask. It's my idea. It's what I want. Anyway, the rent on my apartment is outrageous. Moving in with you would actually be a big help for me."

"Well, if you think you would like it. I could certainly use another pair of hands in the garden."

"The garden will be beautiful, Mom. And we'll clean up the rest of the house too."

"Of course, I do have my things organized in a certain way, dear."

April laughed. "I know you do, Mom." She turned back to Kenji. "How are you with all this, sweetie?"

"I'm not sure. It's not exactly how I was picturing things. What about us? I thought that you and I might move in together at some point."

"Maybe at some point we will." She reached over and took his hand. "I'm not going anywhere."

Kenji shook his head. "Wow, dinner with your family is a real experience."

"Are you going to be okay with this?"

"I trust you to do the right thing. I'm not going anywhere either."

April leaned over and kissed him on the cheek. "I love you," she whispered.

"Are we ready to order now?" the waiter asked, tapping his pencil on the check pad.

They had sex later that night in April's crowded bedroom. Did she really love this man? She watched his smooth back rise up and down with his sleeping breath. Maybe she was scared to fully love Kenji, to fully love anyone or anything. Scared that when you did that, it gets taken away. Isn't that what happened to Margaret? She wanted to sleep now, to still her restless brain, but it kept running on, thinking about the next day, and the one after that. The days when her mother would continue to diminish and Rose would rage on. Kenji said he would wait. But would he? And what about her? What about April? She reached out to touch Kenji's shoulder but stopped short. She didn't want to wake him, wouldn't bother him with her anxieties. Those were hers alone. She slipped quietly out of the bed.

Acknowledgements

First, last, and always I thank my wife, Beverly Stein, who is my chief cheerleader, first reader, and love of my life.

Ciel Downing, a fellow writer and friend, has provided valuable feedback on my writing and encouragement when I most needed it.

Philip Kenney has been an insightful advisor on life and writing, and friend of many years.

Deborah Jayne helped with the arrangement and structure of this book and provided the feedback that I needed.

Andrew Durkin made it all come together. This book couldn't have happened without his expertise.

The Hoffman Center in Manzanita, and specifically their literary journal, provided an early home for some of these stories and an association with other North Coast writers.

The community of Cape Meares—a lovely place to work and live.

The many students I've worked with throughout my

career who have helped and inspired me as much as I hope I've helped them.

I also owe a debt of gratitude to the many wonderful writers of short stories I have admired and learned from over the years. Three that stand out as influences are: Raymond Carver, Alice Munro, and J.D. Salinger. Any similarity between their work and mine is entirely intentional.

About the Author

Butch Freedman was born and raised in Philadelphia, and still considers it his home town, even though he hasn't lived there in over fifty years. He still roots for the Eagles. Now he lives, mostly contentedly and gratefully, on the Oregon Coast with his wife Beverly. Butch has two adult daughters, Jessica and Gabrielle who he loves dearly. A big part of his life has been devoted to writing and teaching. He has published two previous books (*Fancypants: an autobiographical novel* and a collection of personal essays, *Beach Bum: A Life in Pieces*). He has also published many short stories, essays, and memoir pieces. Butch says that "Writing is both deeply satisfying and occasionally frustrating." In his later years, he has become a committed surfer. "When I'm healthy," he will tell you, "you'll find me out in the waves grinning like a kid again."

www.ingramcontent.com/pod-product-compliance
Ingram Content Group UK Ltd.
Pitfield, Milton Keynes, MK11 3LW, UK
UKHW041630190726
13854UKWH00006B/2408

9 798218 489670